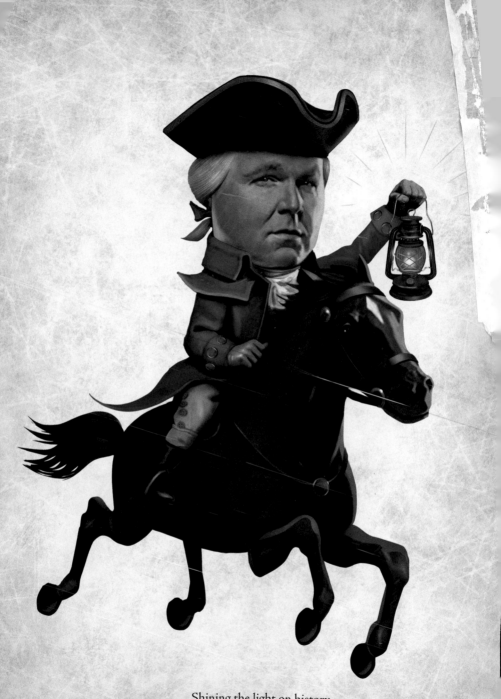

Shining the light on history

Rush Revere

and the

AMERICAN REVOLUTION

*Time-Travel Adventures with
Exceptional Americans*

RUSH LIMBAUGH

with Kathryn Adams Limbaugh

Historical Consultant: Jonathan Adams Rogers
Children's Writing Consultant: Chris Schoebinger
Illustrations by Christopher Hiers

THRESHOLD EDITIONS

NEW YORK   LONDON   TORONTO   SYDNEY   NEW DELHI

Threshold Editions
A Division of Simon & Schuster, Inc.
1230 Avenue of the Americas
New York, NY 10020

First Threshold Editions hardcover edition October 2014

THRESHOLD EDITIONS and colophon
are trademarks of Simon & Schuster, Inc.

For information about special discounts for bulk purchases,
please contact Simon & Schuster Special Sales
at 1-866-506-1949 or business@simonandschuster.com.

The Simon & Schuster Speakers Bureau can bring authors to your
live event. For more information or to book an event contact
the Simon & Schuster Speakers Bureau at 1-866-248-3049
or visit our website at www.simonspeakers.com.

Jacket design by Ariana Dingman
Jacket painting by Christopher Hiers

Manufactured in the United States of America

1   3   5   7   9   10   8   6   4   2

ISBN 978-1-4767-8987-3
ISBN 978-1-4767-8991-0 (ebook)

To the men and women of our great American Armed Forces—
thank you for your sacrifice and commitment to our freedom.

BOSTON

View *of The* ATTACK *on* B
Burning *of* CHARLE

HARLES TOWN

UNKER'S HILL, *with the*
S TOWN, *June 17. 1775.*

Engraved by Lodge.

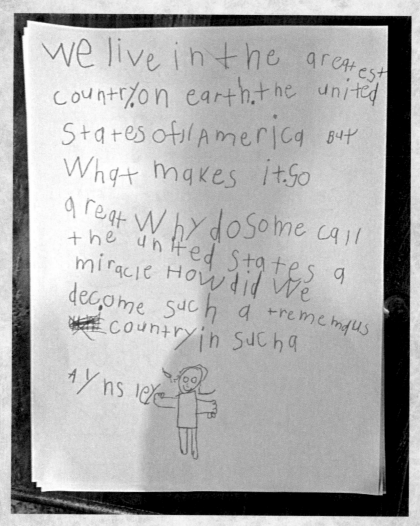

We live in the greatest country on earth. the united States of America But What makes it. so great Why do Some call the united States a miracle How did We decome such a tremendus country in such a

Aynsley

Written by an exceptional young American, Aynsley P.

Foreword

We are fortunate to live in the greatest country on earth. The United States of America is truly the land of the free and the home of the brave. America is an inspiration, a dream for people all over the world.

But how did America happen, how did it come to be? Why are we free?

I often think about these questions and how simply amazing it was that a small group of Patriots could develop a contagious plan that would rally those with the early American spirit to stand up and fight for their independence from Great Britain.

Early Patriot heroes, like Paul Revere and George Washington, were courageous and daring and willing to fight for a cause that was far bigger than themselves. They advanced the mission of the original Pilgrims, who voyaged across rough waters in pursuit of freedom and brought to life a yearning of people since the beginning of time.

Despite the very long odds and being underdogs from the beginning, the American Patriots did not give up. They unified, stood back up every time they were knocked down, and maintained an unwavering belief in God.

Today, we have Patriots serving in our country and around the world as members of our armed forces. We are eternally grateful to these men and women and their families who put their lives on the line every single day to maintain the culture and freedoms that those who came before us worked so valiantly to achieve.

Sit back and get ready to explore this incredible period in history! Rush Revere and his lovable sidekick Liberty are ready to take you on an adventure to meet the American underdogs!

Rush Revere

and the

AMERICAN
REVOLUTION

Prologue

"What are we looking for, again?" asked Liberty as we walked along the dark cobblestone street.

"We wouldn't be looking for anything if you had time-jumped to the right location," I said while forcing a smile.

Don't get me wrong, I felt truly fortunate to have a special horse like Liberty. However, tonight his time-jumping skills were a little off. I stopped walking and glanced around the unfamiliar street, trying to decipher if we were heading north or south. I sighed, took off my hat, and ran my fingers through my hair. I looked up and marveled at the midnight sky filled with billions of stars.

As I tried to find the North Star and get my bearings, I had the strange sensation that we were being watched. I heard something behind us and quickly turned in the direction we had come. "Did you hear something?" I asked.

"If you mean my stomach, yes," Liberty replied.

I pushed the feeling aside and continued walking up the street.

Liberty clarified: "Just for the record, I heard you say, Boston, the Old South Church, April 18, 1775, 9:30 P.M. So that's where I jumped to."

"So is that why we're now *walking* to the Old *North* Church?" I asked. "And through a very dark part of Boston, I might add. It's a good thing I didn't say we're going to the North *Pole*, because you might have heard the *South* Pole instead, and that would've been an even farther walk."

I know it was a simple mistake on Liberty's part but I had planned to meet Robert Newman, a Patriot and caretaker of the Old North Church, tonight at approximately ten o'clock. Hopefully we hadn't missed him.

"I'm just saying I heard you say Old *South* Church," Liberty said. "Maybe you were thinking *north* but you accidentally said *south*. It's like asking you to please pass the salt, when I really meant for you to pass the pepper."

"You don't even like pepper," I reminded him. "Remember, pepper makes you sneeze."

"Oh boy, you shouldn't have made me think of pepper, because now I feel like I have to sneeze." Liberty twitched his nose back and forth and shook his head.

"I didn't make you think of pepper. You're the one who first mentioned pepper."

Liberty sniffed, closed his eyes, and shook his head, but it was too late. Like a shotgun full of snot, Liberty blasted, "Ahh-choooooooooo!"

The sound echoed off the brick buildings and down the cobblestone street.

I turned to Liberty and said, "Bless you." Out of the corner of my eye I could have sworn I saw a dark shadow crossing to our side of the street. "There!" I turned and pointed. By the time Liberty turned around, the shadow had dissolved into a sea of black.

"Somebody's a little jumpy tonight," Liberty said.

Was I seeing things? Maybe the sights and sounds of eighteenth-century Boston were playing tricks on me. "Seriously, I think we're being followed."

"Are you trying to spook me?" Liberty asked suspiciously.

Without answering, I reached over to his saddlebag and grabbed my pepper spray.

"Did you just pull out the pepper spray?" Liberty inquired.

"I'm just being cautious," I stated.

"*Pepper* spray!" Liberty said. "You keep making me think of pepper! Sheesh! You're worse than allergy season!"

"Want a Dr Pepper?" I winked. I couldn't help myself.

Liberty sneezed two more times.

"History is waiting," I said. "We need to hurry."

A whole twenty seconds passed before Liberty asked, "What was I talking about before I sneezed? Oh yes, the Old South Church."

I groaned. "Ugh, I told you we're going to the Old *North* Church. They're both in Boston but they're two different buildings." I took out my smartphone and pushed the icon for the compass app, but I forgot there weren't any satellites in the eighteenth century. "Rats! No service. Let's just keep walking."

"Geez, somebody's grumpy! Actually, somebody's Mr. Grumpy-pants!" Liberty said.

"If I'm grumpy, it's because we're late and we're lost and—"

"And I think that really tall pointy steeple is what we've been looking for," said Liberty.

I turned to see where Liberty was looking, and sure enough, the silhouette of a steeple loomed just across the street. "That's it," I cheered. "The Old North Church." It was an impressive brick building with a majestic white steeple that rose up into the night sky like an angel raising its sword for battle.

As I turned back to Liberty, my smile quickly faded as I saw the shadow of a man in the near distance by a large oak tree. "There!" I pointed. "See him by the tree to the far left?"

Liberty turned and looked where I was pointing. The shadow man just stood there, watching us. Liberty inched backward to stand behind me and said, "Uh, that's creepy. Why is he staring at us?"

"I don't know," I said. "But there's one way to find out." I leapt up onto Liberty's saddle and spurred him forward.

As we bolted toward our watcher in the woods, Liberty said, "I have a bad feeling about this."

More trees came into view as we raced closer. "Which tree did you see him behind?" Liberty asked.

"I thought you knew where he was," I replied. The shadow figure seemed to disappear into the night.

Suddenly, a voice called from the shadows near the church. "Mr. Revere," the voice said. "Over here." The stranger, who looked to be in his early twenties, stepped out from the shadows but did not speak.

"Robert Newman?" I whispered as we walked to where the man stood.

"Yes, good evening sir," Newman replied, waiting for me to speak.

"Thank you for meeting me, Robert," I said. "Paul Revere

asked that I meet you here to help you and the Sons of Liberty. I will assist you in any way I can tonight. Have you brought the lanterns?"

"Yes, sir, I hid the lanterns in—"

Just then two branches crackled, sounding as if someone was walking closely near by.

"Let's be careful," I said, "someone might hear us. The King's spies are everywhere. And the Redcoats are out tonight. They patrol the streets and could pass the church at any moment."

"My apologies, you are right," whispered Newman. "I hid the lanterns in a closet inside the church. The other Patriots will meet us there to help put them in place."

"Well done," I said softly. "Paul will be proud."

"Yes, he told me earlier this evening that General Gage will secretly send the Regulars from Boston tonight to capture Patriots Samuel Adams and John Hancock in Lexington," Newman said as we stood in the darkness. Of course, I knew that when Newman said *Regulars* he meant regular British soldiers, the King's professional army who wore the bright red coats.

If the British army could capture these two American leaders it would be a real blow to the Revolution, I thought to myself.

"We must warn our fellow Patriots across the river in Charlestown. Even now they are watching the tower of the Old North Church for our signal. We decided that if the King's army left Boston by land to invade our other towns we would light one lantern as the sign. But if we discovered his army was leaving Boston by sea, crossing the Charles River, we would light two lanterns," Newman said.

I smiled and said, "One if by land, two if by sea."

"Correct," he answered.

"Come, Mr. Revere," said Newman. "I can get us into the church."

We walked briskly to the front of the Old North Church. The light flickering from a nearby lamppost cast our ghostly shadows upon the white wooden doors. Newman looked left and right as if expecting to see someone.

Newman quickly slipped his hand into his coat pocket and pulled out a large metal key that he inserted into a thin metal hole below the door handle. A loud click sounded as he turned the key. He leaned into the door and it slowly swung open. Newman entered first.

I turned to Liberty and whispered, "You'll need to stay out here. Try to warn us if there's trouble."

"You got it, Captain," Liberty said confidently. "Going into stealth mode in three, two, one." Liberty took a deep breath and disappeared into thin air. His supernatural talents amazed me.

I took one last glance toward the street before entering the church. Did I see a shadow figure move behind a tree? Was it one of the King's spies? It was too dark to tell. I quickly slipped into the church and shut the heavy door.

"Allow me to lock the door behind us; the other Patriots are already inside," Newman said. This time the click of the lock echoed inside the large chapel.

"I'm afraid I can't see anything," I said.

"I will return in a moment, after I retrieve the lanterns and candles," Newman said.

I stood in the drafty, dark room and listened to boots walking across the floor. A door creaked open and I heard the soft click of metal against metal. Before long, Newman's footfalls returned.

"Take my arm and I will lead you to the stairwell," said New-man. "But first, hang one of these lanterns around your neck with this leather strap."

My hands groped in the dark until I touched metal, glass, and leather. Then Newman led me to the stairwell. My fingers traced the walls as we started to climb. The creaking stairs were uncomfortably loud under the circumstances. Inside my head I counted. Ten steps, then twenty, then thirty. After a hundred steps we paused. My legs burned as I tried to catch my breath. Climbing so many stairs was a real workout.

"We must continue," Newman said.

I nodded and continued counting: 110 steps, 120 steps, 150 steps. Certainly, we were high into the church tower. Four more steps and we arrived at the platform at the top of the stairs. It didn't seem as pitch black from up here. I noticed the shape of a ladder in the center of the platform. I assumed it led to the topmost window in the steeple. I could faintly see Newman pull several objects from his pocket.

"What are those?" I asked.

"Flint and steel and a tinder box," he said.

Newman stroked the flint with his steel and before long a stream of sparks sprang onto the dry tinder. Gently, he blew the glowing embers into a flame and lighted the candles. He placed a candle into each of the two square metal lanterns with clear glass lenses.

"The space at the top is too narrow for the two of us. Climb up behind me with your lantern and then pass it up to me when I get to the top," Newman said.

The ladder creaked under our weight. Rung after rung we climbed. We passed large church bells that hung from great wooden beams. Suddenly, Newman stopped above me. Was there something wrong? Was there someone up in the tower?

"I've reached the topmost window. Hand me your lantern," Newman said.

Relieved, I lifted my lantern and handed it to Newman. For only a few seconds he held both lanterns out the northwest window in the direction of Charlestown. I stretched my neck to see the flickering candles burning side by side and I remembered the sign: two if by sea. "We did it!" Newman exclaimed. "Well done!" I said a bit too loudly. My heart was pounding with the excitement of the moment.

"Hurry, we must descend quickly," said Newman, who had already extinguished the candles. "From the top I could see a group of Redcoats heading this way. I don't know if they saw the lanterns. Maybe a spy saw us enter the church and reported us. Either way, we'd better move fast."

Newman handed me the second lantern and I put the leather strap around my neck. Without the candlelight it was uncomfortably dark. As I descended the ladder my foot slipped and I fell to the side. One hand barely grabbed the outside edge of the ladder but the other swung out to the darkness desperate to find something to stabilize myself. My hand pushed up against something metal. I could feel the heavy object swing outward with the force of my weight. Suddenly, I realized it was one of the bells. I stayed my hand to force back the bell that instinctively tried to swing back inward. I cringed at the thought of the sound the bell would make if the clapper struck the metal. As the bell came to a resting stop, the clapper barely tapped the side. I exhaled with relief. With my left arm I pulled myself back to the ladder and tightly gripped both sides.

"That was close," Newman said.

We carefully made our way down to the top platform and then quickly descended the 154 stairs. Newman returned the lanterns to the closet, but upon approaching the front doors of the church we heard voices coming from just outside.

"I tell you I saw someone enter the church," said a gruff voice.

"You also said you saw a horse vanish into thin air!" shouted a second voice. "We are the King's soldiers, not puppets for a spy and a drunkard."

"But I tell you, the horse was right here and then it just disappeared," the spy said.

"Did it have wings?" laughed a soldier.

"Yeah, maybe it was Pegasus. And I bet Hercules was the guy he saw enter the church," said another. It sounded like all the soldiers were laughing now.

"Hurry, this is our chance," whispered Newman. "We can escape out of the church through a window."

We ran through the chapel and climbed up on a bench near a wooden altar. Within minutes, we were up and through the window and standing in the shadows.

"I must return home before anyone notices I am missing," said Newman. "Godspeed, Rush Revere."

As Newman disappeared into the shadows, I looked for Liberty.

"Well, it's about time you showed up," said Liberty. "Do you think the Patriots across the river saw your lanterns? Was the message sent?"

"There you are!" yelled the man with the gruff voice.

Liberty was so spooked by the stranger that he screamed like a girl. The startled stranger nearly jumped out of his boots.

Apparently, the man had never heard a horse scream before. His eyes darted back and forth between us. It was just enough time for me to grab the pepper spray and blast it in the man's eyes.

"Ahhhh!" the man screamed. He covered his eyes with his black-gloved hands and stumbled backward. His black cloak and jet-black hair made him the perfect spy as he disappeared into the blackness.

"You were right that someone was following us," said Liberty. "He saw me disappear in front of the church and then reported you to those British soldiers."

"It might be better if we're not here when he gets his sight back," I exclaimed.

"Sounds good to me," Liberty agreed.

I hoisted myself up onto Liberty's saddle and said, "Let's jump back to the future."

"North or South," joked Liberty.

"Very funny," I said.

"*Rush, rush, rushing from history*," Liberty bellowed.

A small, swirling vortex of purple and gold appeared before us. Liberty galloped toward it as it grew to twice his size. From the corner of my eye I saw the spy trailing us in the distance, a black glove still covering one eye.

Right before we jumped through the time portal, the spy shouted, "I know your secret. I will watch for you. I will find you!"

Chapter 1

You realize we're headed into a military base," said Liberty, a quizzical expression on his face.

I nodded, "Yes, this is the place."

The sign over the gatehouse read MARINE CORPS BASE.

"You're not signing me up for the cavalry, are you?" Liberty asked. "I mean I would look good with a five-star general riding in my saddle, but what about our time-traveling missions to discover the truth about American history? Not to brag or anything, but you sort of need me."

"Yes, Liberty," I said with a smile, "I need you. I'm not enlisting you to join the cavalry. Besides, soldiers aren't fighting mounted on horseback these days. Instead they ride jets and tanks."

"Whew!" sighed Liberty. "So is this a secret mission? Some kind of covert operation with the Marines? Wow! How exciting! Are we getting sent overseas? Will our mission have a code name? Oh, oh, can we call it Operation

Liberty!? And not just because it's my name. Or maybe we need something more abstract, like Operation Butterfly Princess. Too girly? Okay, how about Operation Mashed Potatoes. I mean, who doesn't like mashed potatoes, am I right?"

I laughed at the way Liberty's brain worked. "First things first," I said. "I'll fill you in on all the details after I speak to the guards."

"Got it, Captain," Liberty whispered like he was in commando mode and ready to cross behind enemy lines. "Awaiting your orders, sir!"

I rolled my eyes at his dramatics. Honestly, I didn't have the heart to tell him that I doubted the guards would let him on base. But it was worth a try.

We approached the guardhouse, and two guards stared at me with a penetrating glare. Their camouflage service uniforms looked intimidating, especially with a gun that hung from each of their black utility belts. I got the feeling that not many visitors arrived on horseback and dressed like an early American Patriot. I said, "Hello, I'm Rush Revere and I have an appointment at the base cafeteria."

A guard with a ponytail worn in a tight bun beneath her cap asked, "I'll need to see some identification, sir." She was all business.

I quickly handed her my driver's license. Since Liberty and I had been together I couldn't remember the last time I drove. Why use a car when you have a time-traveling horse?

The Marine turned sharply and stepped into the guardhouse. In a few seconds she returned and said, "Sir, your name is on the approved guest list and your identification checks out." She handed back my driver's license. "However, your costume is highly questionable."

Liberty softly snickered. He still sounded like a horse, but it was obvious he was amused by the guard's comment.

Would they really deny me entrance into the base because of my colonial breeches and stockings? I tried not to sound too defensive and said, "I'm a history teacher, and this colonial outfit is just my way of engaging my students. Now that you mention it, I'm sure I look—"

The guard cut me off and said, "Sir, we have a dress code on base. We wouldn't let someone dressed up like a clown just waltz in here."

Liberty was really enjoying himself now. He huffed and wheezed and shook his head as he tried to choke back his laughter.

The guard glanced at Liberty and asked, "Is your horse all right? He sounds like he's got something caught in his throat."

"Not to worry, he's probably just hacking up a hair ball," I teased.

The guard was not amused.

I smiled and said, "That was a joke, of course. Well, anyway, I'm here to visit a student of mine who lives on base. His mother invited me and felt it was very important that I see him."

The guard paused and then said, "One moment, sir." She returned to talk to the other Marines in the guardhouse.

I quickly whispered to Liberty, "You are not helping matters."

"Sorry," Liberty replied. "But I am curious, do you do birthday parties and bar mitzvahs?" Again, Liberty shook with laughter as the Marine returned from the guardhouse.

"Sir, we'll make an exception for you," said the guard. "But we'll need to pat you down before you enter the base."

"Whew," I sighed. "Not a problem. Thank you very much."

"However, I can't let you enter with your horse. Base protocol."

I could literally feel the air rush out of Liberty. I couldn't blame him. I tried not to let my disappointment show too much and replied, "I understand. No worries. My visit on base won't be long. I'll tie him up to that tree over there and return shortly."

I turned Liberty around and he sluggishly walked across the street to a tree at the side of the entrance.

"You realize how humiliating this is, right?" Liberty mumbled.

"I'm truly sorry, Liberty, but I got a call from Principal Sherman. He told me that Cam's mom wanted to meet me today and that it was important. I have no idea what it is about but I told him that I would help in any way I could." We stood by the tree to talk for a second.

"Ohh! Now I'm worried. I hope it's not too serious. Do you think it's serious? I mean Cam is a total prankster; do you think he got in trouble? Wait, why would she want to meet with you?"

"Ha, if I knew that, I would have told you! Just because I am tying you to a tree doesn't mean I don't trust you," I said with a smile.

"All right, just this once," Liberty consented. "I'll stay here."

Liberty was taking this a lot better than I anticipated. I looked him straight in the eye and said, "Liberty, you understand that you need to stay out here, right? We both know you could easily turn invisible and sneak onto the base without anybody seeing you. Don't think I haven't thought about that."

"What!" Liberty said, sounding shocked. "The idea never crossed my mind!"

"Riiiiiight," I said. "And I bet you also haven't thought about food all day."

Liberty huffed, "Well, I hadn't until you mentioned you were going to the cafeteria to eat!"

"Look," I said, "I promise I'll bring you back something. But we can't afford to have anyone see you on base. Understand? Seriously, I could get into real trouble if those guards find out you're inside."

"Yes, yes, of course, I understand," Liberty said. "Even though I'm a highly trained time-traveling special operative who feels severely underappreciated, I accept the unusual circumstances. And, of course, I would never want to get you in trouble." He dipped his head and raised his eyes like a puppy waiting for a bone.

"Good," I said. "I promise I'll be back as soon as I can. It really shouldn't take long. Here, I brought you something to help pass the time." I pulled out a couple of pieces of bubble gum, unwrapped them, and tossed them into Liberty's mouth.

"Mmm, thank you!" said Liberty as he started to chew.

"Just try not to blow big bubbles. We wouldn't want anyone to see your highly trained, special operative skills!" I winked. "Plus, remember what happened the last time in 1765 when your gum got stuck to the hair of that British Redcoat soldier and it got us all in trouble."

Liberty chewed and replied, "No worries. There aren't any of those mean British soldiers for more than two hundred years from here!" He winked.

"True," I said, "but there are Marines less than two hundred yards away so please behave yourself."

"You can count on me, Captain!" he said with a grin.

After getting patted down by the guards, I found my way to the cafeteria. I entered the doors and noticed plenty of tables and chairs. It was after lunch hour but there were a few Marines and a few families still eating or talking. I made my way over to an empty table and waited for Cam's mom to arrive.

A woman with brown eyes and a tan complexion entered the cafeteria doors. She wore a neatly pressed business suit and several thin bracelets on her wrist. Her dark hair hung neatly around her shoulders. When she smiled I immediately recognized the resemblance to her son.

"You must be Professor Revere," she said.

I took off my hat and replied, "Yes, I am, but I'm only known as Mr. Revere to my students. Please call me Rush."

We shook hands as she eyed my outfit. "Cam told me you usually dress like you're going to Mardi Gras or a Halloween party. He was right!"

"Oh, yes," I said, almost blushing. "Well, I consider it my history uniform."

"I think it looks very dashing," she said, smiling. "By the way, I'm Danielle. Thank you for coming to the base to meet with me. I'm sure this is out of your way."

"It's my pleasure. Anything to help Cam. He's a great student," I said. "He has a real gift for expressing himself. He's a great speaker and his sense of humor is contagious." I smiled at the memory of the fake-eye prank he pulled on his first day.

"Well, he loves your class," she replied. "You've literally made history come alive for him. I mean he's always liked history, but you seem to take it to a whole different level."

"I'm glad to know that," I said, sincerely.

"I don't know how much Principal Sherman told you, but Cam's father was sent overseas to Afghanistan by the Marines last month. Cam took it really hard. He hid inside his closet right before his dad left so they didn't even get to say goodbye. Cam just doesn't get why his dad had to go."

Danielle paused and took a deep breath. "Cam was always such a wonderful kid. He was always so happy and kind. But ever since his dad left, Cam's been, well, let's just say he's not Mr. Wonderful. He's just not himself anymore. Rush, Cam means everything to me. It breaks my heart to see him angry and hurt so much. And I know his father didn't show it, but I'm sure he felt sad that Cam wasn't around to send him off. The thing is, Cam loves his father very much and I know he misses him. But he's put up this wall and won't let anyone talk to him about it. He needs to talk about it. Cam needs to understand why his dad chose to become a soldier. I want Cam to understand the sacrifice his father is making for our family and this country."

Danielle resisted the urge to cry and finally had to wipe away a tear. "I just don't know what to do with him. I've considered sending Cam to live with his grandparents in Atlanta, but I don't know if that would make things better or worse for him." Danielle paused and finally, she said, "The thing is, I think you're the one person who might be able to help. He talks about you and your class all the time. I am so glad I chose to send him to Manchester Middle School. I almost enrolled him at the school on base, but I ran into Principal Sherman at a fund-raiser and he convinced me to send Cam to Manchester."

I nodded. "It's a wonderful school with some amazing students."

"That's what Cam says about you. Amazing! He's says no one's a better teacher. In fact, he talks like he personally knows Patrick Henry from the eighteenth century," she said with a laugh. "Seriously, he says that he and Patrick Henry are tight."

I laughed as well and said, "Well, if you're going to be friends with someone it might as well be an exceptional American, right?"

"True," Danielle said, smiling. "But I think he also feels close to you. In fact, you're the closest thing he has to a father figure right now. Maybe that's why he feels connected to you. Anyway, I thought you might have some ideas on how to help him."

"Cam is a great kid," I said. "I'm not sure what I can do but I'll give it some thought. In fact, where is Cam now?"

"I think he's at the obstacle course. It's not too far from here. Would you like me to show you?" she asked.

I could tell it was more of an invitation than a question. "Absolutely," I said. "It would be great to see Cam again."

Danielle smiled and sighed at the same time. I knew she hoped that I had some magic wand that could make things right with Cam. I wished that I did, but Cam's problems were serious. What was I going to do? It must be so difficult for Cam being without his father.

As we approached the obstacle course I saw several kids, maybe fifteen or twenty, who were taunting and shouting at two boys in the middle of their circle. They looked like an angry mob surrounding two kids in a brawl.

Danielle and I looked at each other at the same time and started racing toward the commotion. Sure enough, Cam was in the middle with another boy who looked much larger and a couple of years older. Behind Cam stood a heavyset kid with rosy red cheeks, sweating. He looked petrified and choked out, "Don't mess with him, Cam, there's nothing you can do. He will beat you to a pulp."

Cam said, "Billy—stop picking on Ed, or else."

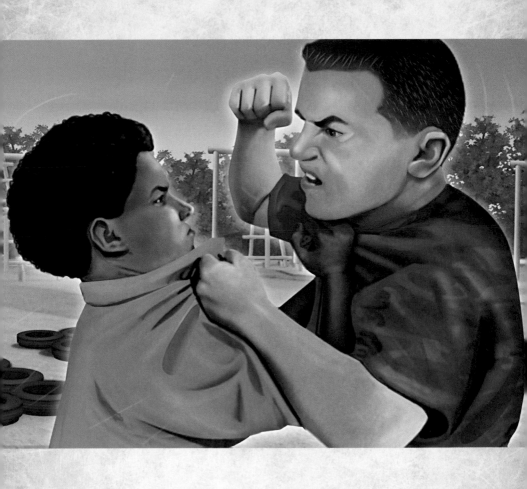

"Or else what?" replied the bigger kid named Billy, who looked like a bully. He had a butch haircut and his fists seemed the size of sledgehammers. "You gonna call your daddy? Oh, that's right, he's not here anymore to save you."

The mention of his dad made Cam grit his teeth.

I could tell Danielle was ready to charge into the middle of the circle so I quickly put a hand on her shoulder. I whispered, "Let's see how Cam handles this."

Reluctantly, Danielle nodded.

Without taking his eyes off Billy, Cam whispered something to the chubby boy named Edward, who then took off running. Cam stood as tall as he could and said, "I don't need my dad to save me. I don't need anyone." Cam brought his fists up in front of him. "Bring it. I've been looking for a punching bag."

"Are you threatening me, punk?" asked Billy with a menacing grin. "You want to mess with me?"

"Why?" asked Cam. "Your face already looks messed up."

"You're dead meat," said Billy, who stepped forward and swung his arm at Cam's head.

Thankfully, Cam was faster and ducked out of the way. Size didn't seem to intimidate Cam as he dove into his larger opponent and swept his lumbering feet out from under him. The Goliath-sized kid landed with a thud and Cam jumped on him like a lion pouncing on its prey. The bigger kid blocked a punch then shoved Cam off. Cam rolled once and then sprang back onto his feet as quick as a cat.

"I'm going to stop this," Danielle said firmly. "I'll be right back." She disappeared behind a building. That's strange, I thought.

I wondered if I should step in and break up the fight. Would that help Cam or not? He certainly wasn't backing down from

Billy. And he made a conscious effort to step in and protect another kid. I gritted my teeth and decided to wait and see.

The boys in the circle continued yelling. Some were cheering for Billy and some were encouraging Cam. Billy took a couple more swings at Cam's head but Cam pulled back just in the nick of time.

"Get him, Cam!" yelled a kid on Cam's side of the circle.

"Yeah, Cam," taunted Billy. "Come on, Cam. Get me, Cam. Is that even your real name? Cam is probably short for Camera. In fact, you should take a picture of yourself looking like a dork."

Cam didn't miss a beat and replied, "Good one, Billy. I bet your name is short for Billy-goat because you smell like one."

Billy charged Cam at full speed. Cam backpedaled but the circle of onlookers blocked his escape and he ended up stumbling and falling onto his backside. Several boys scattered as Billy towered over his prey.

"Now I'm going to teach you a lesson," Billy said threateningly. "The underdog never wins."

Cam was in real danger. I started to run but realized I wouldn't get to him in time to help. Just as Billy leaned over to punish Cam, something hit Billy in the back of the head.

"What was that!" Billy exclaimed as he stood up and turned to see who dared interfere with his fight. No one was there. In fact, all the other boys were lined up on either side of the fight. No one had been standing behind him.

"Who threw that?" Billy yelled as he reached over his shoulder to feel the back of his head. As he pulled away his hand, a mess of sticky, pink goo stretched out from his hair.

"What idiot threw gum into my hair!" screamed Billy.

Gum? Where would a wad of chewed-up gum come from? It dawned on me . . . it had to be Liberty!

Without notice Cam kicked his foot at the back of Billy's legs. Knees buckled and the colossal brute went down hard like a giant tree being cut down.

Cam scrambled to his feet and with an uncontrolled temper he prepared to jump on Billy again.

Suddenly, a blast of water hit Cam in the chest and he stumbled away. Billy was blasted as well. As he rolled over to get up he discovered the dirt had turned into a mud pit. Billy's body was covered in mud, not to mention the gum stuck to his hair, face, and shirt. He really did look like a mess.

Cam yelled, "Mom, what are you doing!"

I turned to see Danielle with a garden hose on full blast. The boys scattered in all directions.

"This isn't over, Camera!" said Billy as he left a trail of muddy footprints behind him.

Finally, Danielle released the handle and the water stopped.

"I can take care of myself!" Cam yelled.

Danielle replied firmly, "Do not yell at your mother. If your father were here—"

"Well, he's not!" shouted Cam. "Remember, he left us! He doesn't care about us!"

"Cameron, you know that is not true," Danielle exclaimed.

"I don't know that. I'm outta here," Cam said, walking away with his chest up. He was shaking his head.

"Cam!" Danielle yelled, but Cam did not turn around.

"Do you mind if I have a talk with him?" I asked.

Danielle nodded.

"Cam, wait up!" I yelled, chasing him. I put a hand on his shoulder.

He shrugged my hand off. "Mr. Revere, I don't need to have a talk with you. I don't care if my mom or Principal Sherman or whoever sent you. I just want to be alone," Cam said, still walking.

"I get it. I know what's happening; your mom told me about your dad."

"You don't know anything!" Cam turned to me, eyes misty and angry.

I looked at him closely and took a deep breath. "No, I suppose you are right. I don't know, but I want to. Will you help me understand?"

"Nope." He smiled a little bit, actually more like a smirk.

Poor kid, I thought. He doesn't know what to do. Suddenly it occurred to me. I don't know much but I do know this—one thing I can do is give him an adventure. Maybe that will take his mind off things.

"Cam, I have an idea. Remember when we time-traveled back to 1765 and met Patrick Henry?"

"Of course, duh," Cam said, "You think I don't have a memory or what?"

"C'mon, buddy." I was trying not to be frustrated with him. I smiled softly and continued: "We had a great time. What do you think? Want to go on another adventure in American history?"

"Whatever," Cam said with a shrug. Then he turned again and ran away.

I walked back to Danielle, who was standing with her arms crossed.

"I'm sorry, Rush. Ie has never been like this. He was always the sweetest boy," she said.

"I understand this must be hard for all of you. I have an idea. I'm going to ask Principal Sherman if I can teach a summer class. I think at least I can get him thinking about something else. Also, it may keep him away from that bratty kid."

"That sounds like a wonderful idea, thank you."

We shook hands and I turned toward the cafeteria. I knew I had to pay off Liberty with a little snack when I got back. Hopefully he was where I left him. As I walked I called Principal Sherman. Lucky for me he always had his cell phone. I asked him about the whole summer class idea.

I passed through the front gate and exited the military base looking for Liberty. I was certain I left him tied to the tree across the street. Did the tree move? Where was he? "Liberty?" I called. No answer. Where could that horse have . . .

"I'm right here," said Liberty, panting.

"Where were you and why are you out of breath?" I asked, suspicious.

"Oh, yes, I am a bit winded," Liberty confessed. "It's, well, it's because I was holding my breath. I was tired of all the people staring and gawking at me in their cars while entering or leaving the base. I felt like shouting, *This is NOT the zoo, people. Move it along!* Sheesh!"

I narrowed my eyes as I pondered his explanation.

"You don't believe me?" asked Liberty.

"Oh, I'm sure that's part of it," I said. "But something tells me I'm not getting the full story. Weren't you chewing a piece of gum?"

"That old stuff," Liberty huffed. "I spit it out ages ago."

"And you didn't enter the base?"

"What kind of question is that?" Liberty guffawed.

"It's a pretty simple question, actually," I stated.

Liberty looked at me like I was thickheaded. He said, "We both know that Marines are required to keep the details of their missions highly confidential. They are sworn to secrecy and live by a code of honor to never divulge information that could compromise the mission."

"You haven't answered my question," I said.

"And I see you brought me back something from the cafeteria," he said eyeing my carrot cake. "But you can eat the frosting. Blech. All I want is the carroty stuff."

I simply shook my head and smiled as I peeled back the plastic wrap, broke off a piece of cake without frosting, and fed it to Liberty. While he was preoccupied eating his cake, I prodded further: "I'm just relieved that Cam didn't get hurt during that fight."

"I know, right?" Liberty said as he stopped mid-chew. "Er, I mean, what fight?"

"Liberty!" I scolded.

"And when were you going to tell me that we were teaching a history course during the summer? Don't I get a choice? I thought we were a team. How are we ever going to trust each other if promises are being made with fingers crossed behind the back?" Liberty sighed, then added, "Not to worry, I've already forgiven you. But seriously, the next time you promise to give someone a shot in the arm of real American history I think you should consult the guy who can get us there. That's all I'm saying."

"And just how long were you eavesdropping on our conversation?" I asked.

"Shh, remember, code of honor." He tried to zip his lips with his hoof.

I shook my head. "Well, Liberty, I spoke with Principal Sherman on my way back here and I have some good news. We will be teaching a summer class with our old time-traveling crew."

"Woo-hoo!" Liberty jumped and kicked with his back hooves. One of the guards looked on with suspicion.

Chapter 2

*I*t was the first day of summer school. I had butterflies in my stomach as Liberty and I arrived
at Manchester Middle School. Would my time-traveling
crew show up? How would Cam react? As we walked into
the school, Liberty held his breath and disappeared. His
skills never ceased to amaze me. The hallway was empty as
we walked into classroom five.

"Liberty!" Freedom shouted as he reappeared. She
jumped up to give him a bear hug, as he snuggled back.

Cam barely nodded at us and then turned back and
slouched in his chair.

As we waited for Tommy, Liberty decided to have some
fun with a *Jeopardy*-style quiz challenge. After the first
couple of questions, Cam was still not very responsive.

"Question number three is for Cam. No pressure but
Freedom is winning two to zero." Liberty cleared his

throat. "What exceptional American said, 'Give me liberty or give me death!'?"

"Oh brother, he definitely knows this one," Freedom said, her hands surrendering.

Cam yawned. "Um, was it the Three Musketeers?"

Liberty raised an eyebrow. "Seriously? I don't think Cam is trying very hard."

Freedom shoved his shoulder, "You know the answer is Patrick Henry. He's your hero."

Liberty piped in: "Remember we time-traveled to 1765 Virginia to meet Patrick Henry, and Cam got arrested and hand-cuffed by the British Redcoats for disorderly conduct? That was crazy!"

Cam shrugged his shoulders.

Liberty tallied the score. "Freedom now has three points and Cam has a big, fat goose egg. Of course, if it was a golden goose egg then you'd be rich! And if you owned a goose that laid golden eggs then you'd be really rich. And if you owned a flock of geese that laid golden eggs . . ."

I smiled while listening to Liberty's random thoughts. I was glad to be back at Manchester Middle School even if it was sum-mertime. I stood by the open window as a light breeze drifted into the classroom and gently blew the American flag. I checked the clock on the wall again and felt a little anxious. Tommy was almost ten minutes late.

Liberty continued: "Of course, if you had an elephant that laid a golden egg, well, that would just be weird."

"I'm sorry to interrupt your insightful conversation," I said, "but has anyone heard from Tommy? He's awfully late."

"I bet he slept in," said Freedom. "Knowing Tommy, he's probably hibernating. It is summer vacation, after all."

Both Freedom and Cam looked casual and comfortable. They both wore shorts and short-sleeve shirts. Instead of the feather I had often seen Freedom wear she had her hair pulled back into a ponytail.

Cam was slumped in his chair with his arms folded. He yawned again and said, "We were gaming at his house late last night. I'd still be sleeping, too, but my mom threatened to bring the drill sergeant to wake me up." He grumbled, "Seriously, she does not pull any punches when it comes to getting me up for school."

Liberty gasped. "Are you saying your mother punches you out of bed? Wow, she's really strict."

"No, it means she doesn't beat around the bush," Cam said, grumpily.

"You have bushes in your bedroom? Boy, you must live in the outback," said Liberty.

"No, I just mean my mom gets right to the point. She doesn't blow smoke."

"Well, I don't blame her," Liberty replied. "Smoking is a really bad habit and is the leading cause of lung cancer!"

Cam pulled his phone from his pocket and said, "Hey, I just got a text from Tommy. He says, 'Sorry, I accidentally slept in. Tell Mr. Revere he better go without me. Don't have too much fun!'"

"That's too bad," I said. "I'm afraid Tommy will miss out on an exciting adventure today. But I want to thank you both for making the effort to come this morning."

"Thanks for inviting us, Mr. Revere," said Freedom, beaming. "This is way better than doing chores."

Freedom turned to Cam expecting him to say something. Instead, he just nodded with his arms folded.

"So will it just be Freedom and me?" Cam asked.

"Yes, only those who have time-traveled before," I said with a wink. Among the three of them, our time-traveling adventurers had landed on the *Mayflower* and met the Pilgrims and Native Americans at the first Thanksgiving. We met Ben Franklin and King George in London, and witnessed the Boston Tea Party. We had even seen fights and angry crowds protesting against the Stamp Tax and saw Samuel Adams get the crowd going. Our next adventure would be even more exciting.

"Uh-oh, does that mean Elizabeth is coming?" Cam inquired.

"I hope not," Freedom said softly. "I don't mean to sound rude. It's just that . . ."

Freedom was too nice to say what she really thought so Cam finished her sentence. "It's just that Elizabeth is a power-hungry, stuck-up, snobbish diva who tries to make everyone around her feel inferior?" He looked around to give Tommy a high five but then realized he wasn't there.

Elizabeth is a student at Manchester Middle School, and the daughter of Principal Sherman. She knew about Liberty and time-traveling and tried to befriend King George when we visited eighteenth-century England. Let's just say she isn't the best-behaved girl in the world.

Freedom blushed. "I wasn't going to use those exact words."

I smiled and said, "No worries, Freedom. Elizabeth won't be attending. Her family is spending a chunk of the summer on the coast. Of course, after the stunt she pulled trying to leak information to King George III I'm not sure I trust her just yet."

"Or ever," Freedom mumbled.

"Let's head outside. The back of the school will give us more room to time-jump," I said.

Both students slipped out of their desks and Liberty opened the classroom door with his teeth. As we walked down the hallway and out of the school I watched Cam out of the corner of my eye. He shuffled along with his hands in his pockets and his head down. This was definitely not the boy I remember playing pranks in class and always smiling.

When we reached the grass behind the school, I thought we should do a little history reminder class, to be sure we were all on the same page. Perhaps it would put Cam in a better mood before we time-traveled!

"Who can tell me what happened when the Pilgrims landed in the New World?" I asked.

"I can!" Freedom said confidently. "They started to build towns and neighborhoods and grew crops on their land."

"Yes, Freedom, you are exactly right!" I said, adding, "The original Pilgrims helped to develop the communities that eventually formed into the thirteen colonies."

"Do you remember why the Pilgrims wanted to have their own colony?" I asked.

"Yes, they wanted to live in a place where they could be free and openly believe in God," Freedom answered immediately after I asked the question.

"Well done, Freedom, you are on a roll!" I said smiling.

"How about you, Cam?" I prodded.

Cam barely lifted his head and said, "Yup. I agree with Freedom."

Cam was not making this easy. But I was not going to settle for grunts and attitudes.

"After the Pilgrims worked very hard to establish the original thirteen colonies, they didn't want anyone coming and imposing strict laws that took away their freedom. When the King of England saw the success they were having in their new communities, he thought the land was rightfully his and should be under his control," I said.

"Cam," I went on, "do you remember how the King tried to show his power and make the thirteen colonies submit to his rule?" I was hoping for more than a yes-or-no answer from him.

Cam lifted his head a little higher and said, "Well, he wanted to show them who's boss by forcing them to submit to tough laws whether the early Americans liked it or not." I nodded, giving him reassurance he was on the right track. "Like the Stamp Act and taxes," Cam said reluctantly.

"Yes, very good! To show his power and try to control the people in the thirteen colonies, the King started to impose tough laws and put heavy fees or taxes on a lot of things sold in the colonies, such as tea. American colonists were also forced to take British soldiers into their homes. That is how the Boston Massacre and Boston Tea Party came to be!" I said.

"Yes," Freedom said, "I remember the Boston Tea Party; it wasn't really the kind of tea party we used to play at my house. They dumped a bunch of tea crates in the harbor to show the King the people weren't happy with all of the fees." Freedom acted out throwing a box over her head.

We spent a few minutes more talking about how the early

Americans had no right to vote and how mad they were that the King shut down the Port of Boston and stopped political meetings from happening.

"The tension in the thirteen colonies only got worse from that point on!" I said. "The early Americans were scared their freedoms were being taken away. Kind of like when you make a big mistake and know your parents are going to get really mad. It's just a matter of time after they find out. Let's go see if we can find out what is happening there now!"

I reached into Liberty's saddlebag and pulled out a colonial dress, a shawl, stockings, breeches, a linen shirt, and leather shoes, among other items, and distributed them to Cam and Freedom. Whenever we time-traveled we did our best to blend into the crowd. It kept us safe and let us fit in with the people of that time. I was already wearing my colonial clothing so I was ready to go.

"Looks like we're going undercover again," Freedom said. She turned to Cam and asked, "Are you as excited as I am?"

"Probably not," Cam said as he began putting his breeches over his shorts.

"Is something wrong, Cam? You don't seem like yourself," Freedom asked.

"Sorry. I'm just, I don't know, I guess I'm just tired."

After they finished dressing in their new clothing I ushered them onto Liberty.

"We need to time-jump to Boston, April 18th, 1775."

"At least it'll be spring and not winter," Freedom said. "I almost froze when we first visited the Pilgrims in Plymouth Plantation."

"Wait," said Liberty. "April 18th, 1775. That's the same date we time-jumped when we last visited Boston. You know, when we were chased by that spy!"

"Yes, Liberty, thank you for that," I said sarcastically. "We are actually heading to Dr. Warren's surgery center on a different street in Boston for exactly that reason. Hopefully, the man in the black coat doesn't find us there."

"You were chased by a spy?" asked Freedom nervously.

For the first time Cam looked genuinely interested.

I avoided Freedom's question and asked my own: "What's your favorite part of time travel?"

"Riding on Liberty through the time portal is the best part. Getting there is half the fun!" Freedom replied.

"Aw, shucks, thanks, Freedom," said Liberty.

"How do you do it?" Cam asked. "I mean I know the lightning storm changed you but what do you actually do to open the time portal?"

"I'm not sure," Liberty replied. "I just say the magic words and think about it really hard and it happens. Before we know it we are back in time to a place in American history."

"It still seems impossible," Cam said.

Freedom sighed. "Oh, Cam. Santa Claus coming down the chimney seems impossible, too, but he does it every year."

"Yeah," said Liberty. "If reindeer can fly then I can time-jump."

I quickly changed the subject before Cam could respond. "Ready when you are, Liberty. I'm right behind you."

Liberty nodded and said, *"Rush, rush, rushing to history."*

The vertical whirlpool of purple and gold appeared between the school buildings. Liberty bolted toward the swirling portal as it got larger and larger. I repeated the date to Liberty and shouted, "The home of Dr. Joseph Warren!" In a blink of an eye we jumped into the eighteenth century.

Liberty landed on the familiar cobblestone streets. It was rather dark out and difficult to determine exactly where we were. We walked under one of the streetlamps. I pulled out an old map of the colonies from 1775 and pointed to where we were in the city of Boston, located on the upper coast of Massachusetts.

Cam said, "Is Boston an island? It looks on the map like it is completely surrounded by water."

"It is very close to an island, yes," I said, "but there is a little strip of land to the south that connects it to the rest of Massachusetts."

We started to walk down one of the cobblestone streets. "I can hardly see anything," Cam said.

"Look, there's the steeple of the Old North Church just a few streets away," Liberty said, looking up and beyond the rooftops. The church was the tallest building in Boston, towering over the rest of the city.

We turned to look where Liberty was staring. A scrawny cat darted across the empty street into an alley.

"Where is the house?" asked Cam.

"Give your eyes a few minutes to adjust to the darkness," I said. "Let's get out of the street and closer to this building. There are British soldiers patrolling the streets tonight. We need to be careful."

"Mr. Revere, why are we being so cautious?" asked Freedom.

"Well, the Revolutionary War is about to start. The Boston Massacre happened not too long ago, and everyone is really angry. Any spark could set off the British Redcoats or the American colonists, and there could be beatings—or worse." Just as I finished a group of British soldiers walked by. *Clank, clank, clank.* Their rifles were held high on their shoulders and their red coats were bright under the lamplights.

"I'm scared, Mr. Revere," Freedom said, curling in close to Liberty. As the soldiers passed we found ourselves next to a neat little house.

"These soldiers are losers; honestly, they treat everybody like dirt and expect us to treat them well. Forget it," Cam said, his voice echoing off the side of the house.

"Let's be careful, guys, keep your voices to a whisper; lots of the King's spies around this house; it's Dr. Warren's surgery," I said.

Liberty whispered, "Who is Dr. Warren, and exactly how can he have a surgery in his house?"

I lowered my voice and said, "Dr. Joseph Warren was the man who organized the midnight ride of Paul Revere. He had many Patriot spies who gathered information for him. And with that information he warned other Patriot leaders about British plans. He helped a lot of people so he kept his surgery at his home. He didn't turn anyone away no matter how sick, or whether they were British or American."

"Wait, was he a doctor or was he a spy? Or was he a spy pretending to be a doctor?" asked Liberty. "Is he working with the awful spy who chased us around?"

"Dr. Warren was a respected surgeon and a leader in medicine in 1775," I said. "But he was also a great Patriot and played a leading role in the early days of the American Revolution. And no, the mean spy works for the King on the British side. Warren is gathering information for the American side."

"I think I see a light inside his house," Freedom said.

"Dismount from Liberty and let's go see if he's inside."

"What should I say or do if I see a spy who is helping the British?" Liberty asked. "I could hoot like an owl. Or caw like a raven. Or maybe I should honk like a goose."

Liberty tried his goose impersonation and the honking sound reverberated down the street.

"Ha! I bet that would get your attention!" Liberty said proudly.

"Yes, it would get the whole city's attention; how about you just tell me?" I firmly whispered.

Suddenly the front door to the house opened and Liberty quickly disappeared. A man's head peered around the side of the door.

"Hello?" asked the man. "Who is there? Are those children? Are you hurt?"

Unsure if the King's spies were nearby and listening, I simply replied, "I regret we have to bother you at such a late hour, Doctor, but this boy needs medical attention."

"I do?" whispered Cam.

"Shh, follow my lead," I said softly.

The man looked up and down the street and then back at us. He finally said, "Quickly, come inside before the King's soldiers spot you." He opened the door to let us in.

I waved for Freedom and Cam to enter the house. As we passed inside the doorway I smiled and said, "I assume you're Dr. Warren?"

"Yes, you have come to the right place. Please bring the boy over to this bed. Let him lie down." Dr. Warren pulled up his sleeves. He looked tired, as though he had been working since five in the morning. His high collar was still buttoned and he wore a linen shirt with ruffles on the cuffs.

In the front room of the home was a bed with a single mattress covered by a linen sheet. Dr. Warren shut the curtains and then moved the lamp from one table to another one closer to the bed where Cam was now lying down. The doctor sat down in a chair next to the lamp.

As he placed his hand on Cam's forehead he asked, "Tell me your name, young man. And what seems to be the problem?"

Before Cam could answer, the sound of boots marching along the cobblestone street invaded the silence. It sounded like a British patrol was passing in front of the home, again. At least I hoped they were passing. Dr. Warren went to the curtained window to get a better look. Freedom's face was pale and her eyes wide. Eventually the heavy footfalls faded away and it was silent again.

"Just some fancy-dressed soldiers prancing and twirling down the streets of Boston," the doctor confirmed with a gentle smile. He was clearly keeping it cool. Dr. Warren placed his hand on Freedom's shoulder and she looked up into his deep brown eyes, which seemed to twinkle. She immediately seemed calmer. Warren then turned to Cam and asked, "Now then, young man, what seems to be the problem?"

I nodded at Cam and hoped he would play along.

Cam swallowed hard and said, "Um, I have a headache, I guess?"

"Yes, of course," said Dr. Warren. "A strong ache in the head can certainly be miserable. Let me prepare you some willow bark tea. I'm sure that will help." He patted Cam on the head gently.

"Cool, thanks," said Cam. Dr. Warren looked up and scratched his head, messing up his neatly trimmed hair.

"Oh, I am sorry; you say you are cool. Interesting, very interesting," Dr. Warren said. He went to his notepad and quickly scanned it.

"No, I mean cool, like it's all good, no worries," Cam said.

"A fascinating expression. Now, may I inquire if you've been inoculated for smallpox? I'm sure you've seen the effects of this horrible disease here in Boston. Early symptoms might include back pain, fever, lesions in your mouth, throat, or nasal passages, and rashes on your skin. Have you experienced any of these?"

Cam shook his head. "Nope, none of that. Just a little headache."

"That is good news. It would be in your best interest to get inoculated while you're here. I will not charge you for the procedure. It won't take long and we will hope for a quick recovery," said Dr. Warren.

"Uh, what?" Cam asked, confused. "Actually, I was just hoping for some Tylenol."

"I have never heard of this Ty-le-nol. If this is a new remedy made from tree bark it might help with your headache but it will hardly cure the effects of smallpox," said the doctor.

Freedom said, "We learned all about the smallpox epidemic in school. It was really sad when Squanto returned to America and discovered that hundreds of Native Americans in his village, including his whole family, had died from the disease."

"Yes, indeed," said Dr. Warren. "And it is beginning to ravage the citizens of Boston as well as the King's soldiers. I dare say it will kill hundreds if not thousands before the end of it. That is why I try to inoculate as many patients as possible." Dr. Warren smiled and patted Cam's shoulder. "Not to worry, young man. I will get your tea and my medical instruments and return in a moment."

As Dr. Warren left the room, Freedom asked, "What's he going to do to Cam? And is he really one of the leaders of the American spy network? He is so nice."

I said, "I'm not really sure what's involved with smallpox inoculation. But I do know that if not for Dr. Warren many Americans and British around Boston would have died of smallpox that year."

"He is really a caring person," Freedom said. "I would like to be like that but with animal patients, like a veterinarian. He could have become ill himself with smallpox. I don't like to see people or animals suffer."

"He also was amazing at organization. He knew everybody in town from the beggars to the aristocrats. He planned the warning system to alarm the people that soldiers were coming to capture our old friend Samuel Adams," I said.

Dr. Warren returned with a silver tray. He placed it on the table next to Cam. Without warning, he pushed up the sleeve on Cam's left arm and reached for a sharp metal instrument from the silver tray.

Cam's eyes looked like they were going to pop out of his head.

"You're in good hands," said Dr. Warren in a warm and compassionate voice. "Now then, this may sting a little. I'm going to make a small incision in your arm and then introduce a mild form of the smallpox disease into the wound. A healthy body like yours has a very good chance of fighting off the disease. When that happens, you'll be immune from smallpox for the rest of your life."

Freedom stood at the foot of Cam's bed and covered her eyes.

"Mr. Revere!" Cam panicked.

I couldn't let Cam get infected with the smallpox, so I stepped up and said, "Dr. Warren, perhaps we should consult with the boy's mother before we . . ."

The doctor gave us a reassuring smile. "I have inoculated hundreds of men, women, and children over the past year. I take very good care of my patients, young and old. This will not be as painful as you think. Take a deep breath. Here we go." Dr. Warren held Cam's arm steady as he moved the surgical knife just inches above Cam's skin.

Just then, the front door opened and a young boy screamed, "Dr. Warren! Dr. Warren! I've got news! The Regulars are on the move!" We heard the front door shut as the boy charged around the corner and entered our room. When he saw us he stopped in his tracks. He looked nine or ten years old, with a coat that seemed one size too big for him.

Dr. Warren released his grip on Cam's arm and gently set down the knife.

Curious, I asked the boy, "You say the soldiers are on the move? Where are they headed?"

The boy's eyes darted back and forth between Cam, Freedom, and me. He hesitated to speak but finally blurted out, "The King's troops are preparing the longboats and heading for—"

Dr. Warren cut him off in a kind but firm tone and said, "Not here. I am treating a patient." He glanced in my direction with concern in his eyes. The fact is I had yet to introduce myself.

I was a complete stranger and for all he knew I could be working for the King's soldiers and lock them all up for treason.

Quickly, I said, "I apologize for not introducing myself earlier. My name is Rush Revere—no relation to Paul Revere! I'm a history teacher traveling with my students, Cam and Freedom. I failed to mention I was given this token by a fellow Patriot." I pulled out the Sons of Liberty coin that Samuel Adams gave me upon my earlier visit. One side of the coin was engraved with a tree and the words *Liberty Tree*. The reverse side had a picture of an arm holding a cap with the words *Sons of Liberty*. It showed I was a true Patriot.

Upon seeing the medallion Dr. Warren exhaled deeply and gave a look of relief.

"All is well," he sighed and then turned to the boy. "I am sorry for acting so suspicious. I wear two hats these days. As a doctor, I am committed to relieving the pain and suffering of anyone who comes to my door. But I am also a passionate Patriot and must fulfill my duty and do all I can to fight against the tyranny of the British Empire."

Dr. Warren smiled, handed Cam a cup of tea, then turned to the scrawny boy and said, "Now then, tell me what news you have."

Eagerly, the boy replied, "General Gage plans to send soldiers to seize Samuel Adams and John Hancock in Lexington and take the ammunition from Concord."

Freedom nudged me. "Who's General Gage?"

"He is the leader of the British army in Boston," I quickly said.

Dr. Warren stared at the boy intently as if considering his options. Suddenly he jumped up and said, "Revere, now is the time to act! We have been planning this for months. We knew the

Do you recognize this exceptional American? Hint—he is the doctor who treated Cam. This is Dr. Joseph Warren. He helped to plan and organize the Massachusetts alarm system including the midnight ride of Paul Revere on April 18, 1775.

What do you think this tool was used for? It is a surgeon's saw used in medicine back in 1776! Can you imagine how different this is from what doctors use today?

King would eventually send his soldiers to take away our freedoms. Now here's the proof." Dr. Warren was pacing around the room, looking at all of us with a fire in his eyes.

He pulled out a map that looked very similar to mine.

"Here. Paul Revere has to go to the wharf at the very north tip of Boston, and row across the Charles River to Charlestown. Then he has to ride as fast as he can about twenty miles west of Charlestown to Lexington and Concord." Dr. Warren pointed to a road on the map. "He must warn Adams and Hancock, before they are taken by the King's soldiers. They are good men, and don't deserve what may happen to them."

"That is so much to remember. What if Paul Revere gets captured?" Cam asked.

"Well, I am glad you asked, Cam." Dr. Warren pulled out a scratched-up notebook filled with little doodles and drawings. "That's where our friend William Dawes comes in," Dr. Warren said. "Dawes is going another way to Lexington in case Paul Revere gets caught or something happens with our first plan. Dawes is going this way over land through Boston Neck."

"Boston has a neck? Does it have a foot, too?" Cam smirked.

"Boston Neck is the small stretch of land south of Boston that keeps it from being an island. It is the only way across by land," Dr. Warren said. "Where was it you said you were from again?"

"Cam was just joking, of course, Doctor. He likes to do that," I said, looking at Cam.

"The time for joking is over, my friends. Now we must act," Dr. Warren said.

"What can we do to help?" Freedom asked, her eyes as bright as Dr. Warren's.

He smiled and wrapped an arm gently around her shoulders

and faced us. "Do all you can for liberty, and never give up, no matter the sacrifice. Freedom is the basis of all things. Without it we have nothing." Dr. Warren looked deep into Freedom's eyes. "No matter what happens, my strong young friend with such a fitting name, whatever happens, don't ever give up. We have so much to do for the future of our country."

Dr. Warren turned and walked briskly to his desk by the curtains, his shoulders pulled back and his face serious. He sat down in a chair, pulled out pieces of parchment, and quickly scratched a note with his quill pen. He signed it, sealed it, and handed it to the boy.

"Do you know William Dawes?" asked Dr. Warren.

"Yes, sir," said the boy.

"Take this letter to him. Once the letter is delivered I want you to race to Paul Revere's home and tell him to come at once. It is a matter of life and death."

The boy didn't respond but turned and rushed out of the room and out the door.

Within minutes, the door flew open and Paul Revere strode into the room. He seemed full of nervous energy and he wore a heavy coat and three-cornered hat. He was as strong as I remembered him.

"I knew I could count on you, Paul," said Dr. Warren. "Do you know Rush Revere?"

"Of course," said Paul with a wide grin. "I am always glad to see you. Hello, my young friends."

Freedom smiled. Cam nodded. Dr. Warren repeated the information that the boy spy shared.

"Okay, I understand, Dawes is going around Boston Neck,

and I am going over the Charles River," Paul Revere said, looking at Dr. Warren's map.

"Yes," said Dr. Warren. "But be careful. I hear reports that every road is filled with soldiers looking to lock up Patriots."

Paul nodded and said, "Yes, sir, we took care of that. I met with Newman at the Old North Church earlier. He can see all of Boston from there. If the Redcoats come by land he will hang one lantern. If they come by sea he will hang two lanterns."

"Who cares if you hang lanterns anyway? What difference does that make?" Cam asked.

"It's important because the people across the river in Charlestown are looking at the Old North Church to see the signal. Once they see the lanterns they will prepare a horse for Paul Revere and start the warning system. If one system fails, another goes on," Dr. Warren said.

"Yes, and I will cross the Charles River to the other side, under the cover of darkness. If all goes well I won't be captured by the King's warships," Paul said.

"How are you getting across the river?" asked Freedom.

"I have a small boat, hidden beneath a wharf on the waterfront, in the North End," said Paul. "If all of you are willing to help I will meet you there shortly. Your eyes and ears will be especially helpful tonight."

"We are ready to join you and help in any way we can," I said.

At that moment Paul Revere ran out the door and said, "Meet me at the wharf on the North End. Let's go separately in case any of the King's spies are around."

"That sounds good; we will leave in five minutes and see you there," I said.

"Will you be going with us, Dr. Warren?" Freedom asked.

"No, one of us must stay in Boston at the home base," said Dr. Warren, smiling. "There is much to do. I will meet you again soon. I will be wherever I am needed most for the cause of freedom."

"Please be safe," Freedom said.

He smiled and said, "Godspeed. Stay safe, my friends. So long."

Freedom surprised me by hugging Dr. Warren and he smiled kindly. He put out his hand and said, "Thank you for helping with the cause." Cam looked down and shook this exceptional American's hand.

As we exited the home, Liberty whispered, "We're being watched. A man slipped behind the corner of that building as soon as you opened the door."

"Good to know," I said. "Watch out for him."

We quickly left on Liberty, trying to avoid the King's spy as we snuck down the road and chased after Paul Revere.

Liberty accelerated and galloped into the blackness. After about ten minutes he whispered, "I think we're approaching the North End. Keep a lookout for Paul Revere."

"Where did he say he hid the boat, again?" Cam asked.

"He didn't," said Freedom. "He just said it was the North End."

"No worries," I said softly. "Remember, we're riding a GPS that can track historical heroes. Liberty, what do your time-travel senses tell you about the location of Paul Revere?"

Liberty answered, "He's very close. Coming this way, probably to the wharf in front us."

"Let's all dismount," I said.

"Speaking of GPS, that reminds me I need to answer the call of nature, if you know what I mean," Liberty said with a wink.

"You realize GPS stands for Global Positioning System," I clarified.

"Oh, really? I thought it stood for Gotta Pee Soon," said Liberty. "Be right back."

Seconds after Liberty trotted away Paul Revere appeared out of the darkness from the opposite direction.

"Come down to the waterfront with me," said Paul. "There should be two other Patriots waiting for us near the boat who will help me row to Charlestown. You can help us push off. By the way, didn't you have a horse? I thought I saw it outside Dr. Warren's house."

"Oh, yes," I stammered. "Um, my horse, Liberty, is close by."

Paul nodded and then looked at Cam and Freedom. "Would the two of you be willing to stay here and alert us if you hear any Redcoats approaching or see any spies lurking about?"

"Why not?" Cam said.

"I guess," Freedom reluctantly answered.

"If you hear or see anything suspicious, run down to the boat and tell us," said Paul.

"No problem," said Cam. "Come on, Freedom. We can watch from behind those wooden barrels."

Paul and I briskly walked to the water's edge. The sound of water lapping against the wharf made it feel like it was just another night. But something in the air gave me the chills.

At the waterfront two men were waiting. A look of worry and consternation covered their faces. They silently pointed to the harbor. Looming in the distance was the ghostly outline of a very large ship.

Paul stared with solemn eyes. He leaned close to my ear and softly said, "It is His Majesty's ship *Somerset*. General Gage is determined to keep us from crossing and warning the people in the countryside."

"Will you try to leave Boston by land?" I whispered back.

"No, we will proceed with Dr. Warren's plan. It is unfortunate that the warship is directly in our path. No coincidence, I am sure."

I questioned the decision to continue the mission and said, "Surely the King's troops on that ship will see you passing."

"Our plan is set in motion," said Paul. "We knew the odds were not in our favor. They have never been in our favor. But we do not need odds when God is in our favor. I will attempt the crossing. God willing, the impossible will be made possible."

I nodded in awe and wonder at the faith and steadfastness of Paul Revere. He was one hundred percent committed to the cause of freedom. They knew they were the underdogs but it did not stop them from fighting for their beliefs.

Paul whispered, "There is no time to spare. Let us grab the boat and carry it into the water."

Hidden beneath the wharf was a small boat and two long oars with cloth over them. I knew they added the cloth to muffle or quiet the sound of the oars on the water as they rowed. We placed the oars inside the boat and carefully carried it into the dark river.

"Look," said Paul Revere as he pointed back toward Boston.

Suddenly I heard footfalls coming in our direction. I turned and saw Cam and Freedom running toward us, waving and pointing behind them.

Chapter 3

*M*r. Revere!" *Freedom* screamed as she yelled from their lookout point, "Someone is coming—we think it's a spy!"

Oh no, I thought, exactly what I hoped we would avoid.

Hearing the commotion, Paul jumped into the waiting boat with two boatmen. They turned toward Charlestown and placed their oars in the dark water.

"Thank you, Rush Revere," Paul Revere said. I shoved the boat as hard as I could and ran back toward Cam and Freedom. When I got back to them, the spy cornered us against the wharf.

"Who are you and what are you doing here?" asked the spy angrily. "In the name of the King I demand an answer."

Cam was sticking out his chest toward the spy and his face was serious and angry. It reminded me of the fight with the bully, and it worried me.

"We are just here to fish," I said, the first thing that came to mind. Cam and Freedom looked at me quizzically. I glanced sideways toward the Charles River and saw that Paul Revere's boat was still close to shore. If the spy saw him we were all in trouble.

"Yeah, we are fishermen," Cam repeated, "and you look ridiculous in your cloak. Who do you think you are—James Bond?"

The spy raised his gun and said, "You are clearly not fishermen. To begin with, you have no fishing equipment." At that moment the spy looked up toward the river and seemed to see something.

"What is that?" he said, pointing to the water. I could see the shadow of the boat, but the moon was playing tricks on the water so the picture was coming in and out. What could clearly be seen, though, was the huge boat in the middle of the river in Paul Revere's path.

"Oh, that. That is HMS *Somerset*, I believe, sir," I said, knowing full well he meant the small boat with Paul Revere.

"Not that, you fool, the small boat rowing across the river." I could now see the spy held a pistol with a black barrel and mahogany base. Although it was probably close to midnight, the nearly full moon that hung low to the horizon made me feel like we were all actors on center stage, except there would be no audience to witness my dramatic death scene.

"You must be seeing things," said Cam. "There's only one big boat but no small one."

With the barrel of the pistol pointing at me the spy sneered, "Keep your hands where I can see them. I should shoot you where you stand and throw these children in jail."

I moved in front of Cam and Freedom, who looked frightened. Liberty, returning from his bathroom break and acting like a true horse, sauntered up to us and looked surprised.

The man quickly glanced at Liberty and said, "I don't remember seeing a horse on the wharf. Bring him to me, slowly."

Suddenly I had an idea. We had to distract the spy until Paul Revere made it across the river or everything would be lost. I hoped Liberty would play along. I imagined the wharf as a stage and the moon a giant spotlight. I was determined to make my seventh-grade drama teacher proud. I turned to where Liberty was standing but looked past him like he wasn't there. I continued turning and searching until I completed a 360-degree turn and was once again facing the spy. Looking confused, I shrugged my shoulders and asked, "What horse?"

Again the man glanced at Liberty. He looked at me like I was a complete idiot. "I don't know what kind of game you are playing. The horse is right there," he said, and pointed. "I can see it as plain as—"

The spy stopped midsentence, mouth opened, and stared at Liberty, who was now trying to wave a hoof. The spy just stood there, dumbfounded. Then Liberty took a deep breath and disappeared. The timing couldn't have been more perfect. Liberty always had a flare for the dramatic. He loved the theater and always dreamed of starring in the Broadway productions of *Fiddler on the Horse* or *Little Shop of Horses* or *The Phantom Horse of the Opera*. Of course, now he was giving an Academy Award–winning performance of *The Phantom Horse of the Wharf*.

"Where did . . . how the . . . what is going on!" the spy demanded.

Liberty reappeared on the other side of me and waved at the spy, again. For a second time, he inhaled and disappeared. Needless to say, Liberty's phantom-horse trick got the spy's attention. His head jerked back and forth, eyes searching frantically.

"Is everything all right?" I asked with fake sincerity.

"I'm confused," the spy said. I could see in the distance Paul Revere going under the massive hull of the huge *Somerset* warship. A British soldier in red paced the deck above Paul Revere's small rowboat, guarding the *Somerset* and keeping a lookout. It seemed impossible for Paul Revere to make it across safely without being seen!

"Mr. Revere, I'm really scared," whispered Freedom.

"Stop talking," the spy exclaimed. His brow furrowed and his eyes wandered aimlessly. He spun around quickly as if to catch someone sneaking up behind him, and then a second later his pistol was once again pointing in our direction. He finally said, "Maybe it is the moon playing tricks on me. I need to orient myself."

"For the record," I clarified, "you are in Boston, 1775."

"I know where I am!" the man said with contempt. "I know these streets. I patrol them every night by order of General Gage."

Again, Liberty appeared right in front of me. But this time he moonwalked on his back legs across the wharf.

"There it is again!" The spy panicked and pointed. "How is that possible? Surely, you see it!"

Cam and Freedom quickly caught on to what was happening and tried to ignore Liberty as he walked forward while gliding backward. At the end of his moonwalk he spun around once and then lifted one hoof to his mouth like it was a smoking gun and pretended to blow it out. Liberty winked and again vanished into thin air. Priceless, I thought.

The spy rubbed his eyes with his fingers and shook his head.

I cleared my throat and said, "Clearly, there is no horse on the wharf."

The spy pressed his fingers against his temple. He squinted as if he were struggling to see and said, "That does not explain why you are here. I know the rebel Patriots use children as spies."

Cam laughed and said, "We're not spies. But to be honest we're not fishermen, either. We're ghost hunters. We heard this wharf is haunted by a phantom horse who hunts the King's spies in the dead of night."

For the first time, Freedom smiled and had to cover her mouth for fear of laughing.

I pressed my lips together and pinched myself.

The spy acted unnerved. He twitched as he scanned the wharf again, trying to anticipate where the phantom horse would appear next.

Suddenly Liberty appeared inches from the spy's pistol. He wrenched it from the man's hands with his teeth and tossed it into the water. Then he stared the spy straight in the eye and in his best Count Dracula voice he said, "I want to suck your blood."

The spy yelled with pure terror and turned running in a full sprint. Liberty gave chase and galloped behind him, his muzzle just inches from the man's neck. The final touch was Liberty's wicked laugh, which gave even me the chills.

"Do you think he'll come back?" asked Freedom.

"Doubtful," I chuckled. "He's probably halfway to Virginia by now."

Before long, Liberty returned.

I raised my eyebrows and asked, "Really? *I want to suck your blood?*"

Liberty shrugged. "I was in character. I think the vampire, phantom ghost thing really worked for me, don't you?"

"I liked when you moonwalked," said Cam. "I did not see that coming. At all."

"Did you guys see if Paul Revere made it to the other side?" Freedom asked.

"No, I saw him right as he was about to go under the massive ship and then he disappeared," Cam said.

"Mr. Revere, we have to go help him. Dr. Warren asked for our help," Freedom said.

"But we can't cross the river and catch him; we don't have a boat," Cam noted.

"We won't go in a boat," I clarified. "We'll time-jump. But first, I propose we jump back to modern day."

"Good idea," said Liberty. "I need a snack, and some lunch, and an after-lunch snack."

Cam and Freedom hoisted themselves up onto Liberty's saddle, and I encouraged Liberty to open the time portal.

Like the magic words from the story of Ali Baba and the Forty Thieves that opened a secret cave, Liberty spoke the magic words that opened the mouth of the time portal: *Rush, rush, rushing from history.*

We ran toward the swirling vortex of purple and gold and jumped through, landing back at Manchester Middle School.

We arrived just seconds after we had left and in the same location—the back of the vacant schoolyard. It was still about 10:15 A.M. A few grasshoppers jumped away from us in the warm grass.

"Thanks again, Mr. Revere. Thanks, Liberty. You two are the best," said Freedom.

"Yeah, traveling back in time and almost getting thrown in jail by a British spy is a lot better than being stuck at the base," Cam said. He sighed. "Ugh, not sure what I'm going to do now. Maybe I'll drop by Tommy's house and see if he can hang."

"If he's not still sleeping," teased Freedom.

"Mr. Revere, could I ask you a question before we go?" Freedom asked.

"Of course, what is on your mind?" I said.

"Well, um, are we going to go back and see Dr. Warren again on our time travels? Yunno, I think I really want to be a veterinarian and I think he could teach me a lot about taking care of patients, even if they are the furry kind," Freedom said. "I really liked how he took care of everyone, even at his own house. I would like to do that. I would have birds, and dogs, and horses, and cats, and frogs, and turtles, and wombats, and fish, and . . . did I say turtles? I really want to ask Dr. Warren how he does all of that at his house. What if the British find out and take him away?" I don't think I heard Freedom put that many words together in a sentence before.

"Yes, we should plan to go back and see him again soon. He was a big part of the founding of this country!" I said, knowing she was hoping I meant return right this minute. It was interesting how she equated Dr. Warren's compassion for people with her own for animals. Of course, she was the only one I knew who could speak telepathically with Liberty.

"I'm a big sports guy," Cam said as his eyebrows rose. "Dr. Warren reminds me of a head coach who drafts a bunch of good players to be on his team." He seemed proud of his comparison.

"You know, Cam, you are exactly right. In many ways, Dr. Warren helped to put together America's first team to fight back against the British team. He organized the game strategy and who would do what, when, and where," I said, encouraging Cam to keep going. "You could say that America was just starting to put together its team."

"Yeah, like a draft," Cam said in his best deep sports commentator voice. "America's Team is on the clock . . . we pick Paul Revere in the first round . . . a strong Patriot out of Boston . . . Yes!"

"Too bad Tommy is missing this," I said. "He would love to know that you turned history into a football draft. Now, that is cool." I was happy to see Cam a little more energetic than he had been in a while.

"Do you think that William Bradford and the original Pilgrims would play on Dr. Warren's American Team?" Freedom asked.

"Great question, Freedom. William Bradford, the Pilgrims, Patrick Henry, Ben Franklin, Samuel Adams . . . they were all great Patriots even though they lived during different times. Dr. Warren would definitely put them on his team if he could." I was thrilled with their creativity.

"The Pilgrims really started all of this when they came over on the *Mayflower* to start their own free colony, away from the King of England. So maybe we should say they were the inspiration for America's Team. Almost like a mascot."

Liberty smirked. "Pilgrims makes me think of the first Thanksgiving, which makes me think of corn, which makes me hungry, hint-hint."

"Oh, yes, Thanksgiving. I loved that time-travel adventure. Squanto taught me how to plant corn and then we all got together with the Wampanoag Native Americans and the Pilgrims for a huge feast," Freedom said.

"Hey, the first Thanksgiving was kinda like the first team meal. I mean not all the American first-rounders were there yet, but it works." Cam laughed for just a second.

"You know what else works: my stomach," Liberty piped in. "Seriously, it works overtime when we time-travel."

"Real smooth, Liberty," Cam laughed.

"Hey, speaking of smooth," Liberty said, "how about we all go and get some smoothies? I'm craving a strawberry, asparagus, spinach, oats, and alfalfa smoothie! I think you'd really like it."

Freedom gently replied, "Oh, um, thanks, Liberty, but I think I'll just stick with the strawberries."

"Smoothies sound like a wonderful idea," I said. "My treat. How about you, Cam?"

"Sure, I guess," said Cam with his hands in his pockets.

On our way there Liberty tried to talk us into tasting alfalfa. "Seriously, it's pretty good but it's not the same as clover. But if you really want to try the good stuff you should get the beet pulp. Now that stuff will put hair on your chest!"

After our smoothies, minus the alfalfa and beet pulp, we headed for the military base. Before long, we arrived at the front gate and Cam jumped down.

"Are you sure you want to take me home?" asked Freedom. "It's several miles from here."

"Trust me," Liberty said. "I'd much rather get the exercise than be tied up to a tree." He glared at me from the corner of his eye.

"I don't make the rules," I said. "The Marines at the front gate said no horses on base."

Cam kicked a rock down the street and said, "Mr. Revere, I can walk home by myself. You don't need to come with me. I am not a baby, you know."

"It's not a problem," I said. "I'm happy to walk with you."

Freedom waved goodbye and Liberty said, "Cheerio! Actually, a bowl of Cheerios sounds really good about now." Freedom guided Liberty and they cantered away.

Gratefully, the Marines at the guardhouse did not give me a hard time about my outfit when I entered the base. As Cam and I walked to the cafeteria he said, "My mom thinks I'm going to get into a fight, doesn't she? That's why she asked you to walk me home and stay with me until she got home."

I pondered about how I should respond and replied, "Cam, I'm honored that she'd ask me to accompany you. It sounds like she's more worried about other kids than you. And it's really not a problem. Besides, I trust you would make the right choice if you were ever confronted again."

When we arrived at the cafeteria Cam asked, "So you trust that I won't get into a fight?"

Was this a test? I thought. I decided it was and replied, "Just to be clear, sometimes fighting is necessary to defend our families and our freedoms. Sometimes fighting is necessary to stop tyranny and bring peace. That's why your dad chose to serve in the military. But there are other times when fighting is senseless. I believe you know the difference, Cam. So, yes, I trust you."

Cam stared at me and finally replied, "Well, then since you trust me, I'd like to be alone for a little bit. I need some time to think."

How could I say no to that? Then again, I did tell Cam's mom that I would watch after him. But what if he got into trouble on my watch? I doubted Cam's mom would trust me much after that. I decided to go with my instincts and said, "Yes, of course. I completely understand the need for some alone time. But since

I did tell your mom I'd be here for you, I'll just wait here in the cafeteria. I can use the time to map out our next time-travel adventure. You know where to find me if you need me."

Cam nodded and waved. He exited the cafeteria and turned right.

If only I had the ability to turn invisible, I thought. Did I really trust Cam? Mostly. I waited a few more seconds before I bolted toward the door, slowly opened it, and peered to the right just in time to see Cam enter the next building. My curiosity got the best of me so I slipped out of the cafeteria and hid in the shadows of the buildings. I peered through a side window that was open halfway. I noticed that Cam was in a gym filled with treadmills, stationary bikes, weightlifting equipment, and even punching bags. Cam had taken off his shoes and was strapping a pair of boxing gloves to his hands. Within a couple of minutes he was wildly punching the bag with jabs, hooks, and even some roundhouse kicks. Punch after punch he grunted and gritted his teeth. Obviously, he was releasing some frustration. After an intense three minutes Cam came to a rest, breathing hard.

The outside door to the gym opened and the last person I wanted to see entered the building. Billy the bully walked in wearing shorts and a tank top. He was even bigger than I remembered. He immediately recognized Cam and headed in his direction. This is exactly what I hoped to avoid.

Cam must have heard Billy approach because he turned around and stopped to see what Billy was up to.

"Well, look who we have here," said Billy. "Cam and a punching bag. It's hard to guess who will win, since neither of you has any brains."

Cam didn't reply. Instead, he tightened the straps on his boxing gloves.

"No stupid comeback? Maybe you do have some brains," taunted Billy. "Or maybe you're just too afraid to say anything since your daddy isn't around to save you."

Cam paused without looking at Billy and then starting jabbing and striking the punching bag. I was impressed by Cam's self-control.

"You hit like my grandma," Billy mocked. "What are you trying to do, get big and strong 'cause your daddy can't protect you?"

Cam swung his leg with a fierce roundhouse kick that sent the bag swinging into Billy. Cam grinned slightly as Billy stumbled backward.

"Sorry about that," Cam said unapologetically.

"Whatever," Billy said. "You know you want to hit me. Go ahead. Give me your best shot." Billy raised his hands and stuck out his chest. "Nothing? Really? I don't blame you. You're too weak and scrawny to mess with this!"

Cam rolled his eyes. "Whatever."

Billy got awkwardly close to Cam's face and said, "Come on, let's go!"

Cam stepped away and said, "I'm not going to fight you, Billy, but I will compete against you—my team versus your team. Let's say next week."

"You're on," Billy said. "I'll beat you in any challenge. It's almost not fair but I never back down from a challenge."

"Good, then I'll text you when and where," said Cam.

"Oh, one more thing," said Billy. "When you lose, you and your whole team will have to wear T-shirts for the rest of the year that say LOSER on the front in big, bold letters. Every day, every hour, and every minute I want you to remember the humiliating loss. In fact, I'm going to invite the entire base to the competition so everyone can see you lose. Well, except your daddy. That's okay, you can send him a postcard that says, 'I'm the king of losers!' I can't wait!" Billy turned around and laughed all the way out of the gym.

Cam started wailing on the punching bag again. Striking, kicking, kneeing, punching like never before. He was relentless as he pummeled the bag and then gave one final right hook and pushed off until his back hit the wall and he slumped down to the ground from sheer exhaustion.

I decided it might be a good idea to give Cam some time to cool down. As I walked back to the cafeteria I thought about Cam's confrontation with Billy. It could have ended badly in the gym, but Cam remained in control. He chose not to give into his anger and not to engage in a fight. Of course, it would be extremely humiliating if Cam lost this challenge. Billy looked like a mighty opponent.

Cam and his team would certainly be the underdogs. How could he win? Cam had some major planning to do.

Chapter 9

A new morning brought overcast skies to Manchester Middle School. Cam, Liberty, and I stood behind the school on the grass near the track, waiting for Tommy. This had become our time-travel meeting spot.

"Hey, Mr. Revere. I made it!" shouted Tommy as he jogged up to us. "Hey, where's Freedom?"

"She texted this morning and said she had some family stuff," I replied.

"I think she's still recovering from our adventure," said Cam.

"For sure, we found ourselves in some intense moments. Freedom and Cam were very brave, especially Cam," I said. "He had nerves of steel in Dr. Warren's home."

"I heard about that," exclaimed Liberty. "Dr. Warren almost intoxicated him for smallpox."

"Not intoxicated," I corrected with a chuckle. "Inoculated."

"Ahhhhh!" said Liberty, grinning.

"I'm just glad that's over. I've never been a big fan of sharp knives just inches from my skin," Cam clarified.

"Sounds like I missed a great field trip! So where are we heading this time, Mr. Revere?" asked Tommy.

I fed Liberty a crisp carrot from his saddlebag and said, "I was thinking we should go and see if we can follow Paul Revere. We need to see if he made it across the river."

"Sounds good to me! But you need to fill me in on the river crossing part," said Tommy.

"Okay, I'm in," Cam chimed in. "Hanging with you guys is safer than sticking around the base."

"Is that bully still bothering you?" asked Tommy with a half smile.

"Yeah. And I sort of challenged him to a competition," said Cam.

"Seriously?" Tommy asked, raising his voice. "You really are brave. Stupid, but brave."

"Thanks, dude. I'll let you know when I need some backup. It could get dangerous," replied Cam with a smirk.

"So can the bathroom after my dad uses it," joked Tommy.

I smiled and nodded. "All right, then. Liberty, I think it's about time we jump. Boys, change quickly into your colonial gear."

Liberty swallowed the carrot he was chewing and asked, "Where are we going?"

"We're time-jumping to the other side of the Charles River, to Charlestown, directly across the water from Boston's north tip," I said.

Liberty nodded. "Got it, Captain. Are we jumping to April 18th, 1775, again?"

A modern-day view of the Old North Church in
Boston, with a statue of Paul Revere in front.

"Correct," I confirmed, "about eleven o'clock at night somewhere near the Charlestown shore."

Liberty took a deep breath and said, *"Rush, rush, rushing to
history!"* He started forward and was soon galloping toward the
purple and gold time portal that was now swirling in front of us.
I ran behind Liberty as Cam and Tommy clung to his saddle.

We landed in a grove of trees not far from the river. Nearby,
there were some brick houses with chimneys, but Charlestown
looked much smaller than Boston. I turned around to see the
wide Charles River behind me. I could clearly see the Old North
Church across the water as I looked back at Boston. I explained
to Cam and Tommy that Charlestown was almost an island it-
self, similar to Boston, and thus we were surrounded by water on
one side and hills on the other.

It was late at night and dark, but we could still see the huge
warship *Somerset* in the moonlight. It still guarded passage between Boston and Charlestown. The ship was so close I could
hear the massive hull tugging at its huge anchor. Even the voices
of the British Redcoats on board could be heard as bits and
pieces of their conversation drifted across the water.

Whispering, I said, "We need to find Paul Revere. If he made
it past the warship, he should be on this side of the river about to
go on his Midnight Ride."

"Let's find out," said Tommy, who yelled, "Hey, Paul Reve—!"

Quickly, Cam silenced him with a hand over his mouth.

"Shh, someone's going to hear us," Cam whispered.

"Cam's right," I said softly. "We need to stay quiet. We can't let
anyone know we're here. General Gage ordered several soldiers

on horseback to patrol these roads and stop anyone who looks suspicious."

"Oops, sorry," whispered Tommy. "Now I get why Freedom freaked out. The British soldiers could be hiding behind any one of these trees and could throw us in jail . . . just because!"

This is exactly why Dr. Warren planned everything so well. He made sure there was more than one rider and they spread the alarm in every town they passed. This meant that if one rider was captured, the others could go on.

"I sense another horse just beyond those trees," said Liberty. "It's too dark to see from here but I'm sure of it." Just as we started to head in that direction to get a closer look, a single figure on a dark horse came galloping by us.

"Whoaa," said Cam, startled by the speed.

All of a sudden the horse stopped, turned around, and started walking toward us. Oh no, I thought, this isn't going to be good. As the trees cleared I could see the face of the rider. It was Paul Revere.

"Paul, it's me, Rush Revere!" I yelled out.

"Rush, I knew it had to be you. I thought I saw a boy but I wasn't sure so I came back for a quick look. I am so glad that you made it across." Paul Revere dismounted next to us.

"The guard on the big ship didn't see you!" Cam said with excitement.

"No, we were very lucky indeed. Somehow with the angle of the moon and the fog, the soldiers on the warship *Somerset* could not see us crossing below," replied Paul.

"Where are you heading now?" I asked.

"I am following Dr. Warren's plan. First I have to let the

people in the countryside know about the King's soldiers coming. They'll need to get ready and armed to protect themselves."

"What happens if they don't have time to get ready?" Cam asked Paul.

"If the people are caught off guard, the Regulars will come in, capture our Patriot leaders, and take all of our gunpowder," Paul said, adjusting his saddle. "The Patriots in Charlestown saw the two-lanterns signal at the Old North Church across the river and knew it was time. I am thankful to Deacon Larkin for getting this wonderful horse called Brown Beauty ready for the ride."

Liberty perked up at her name, and turned his head toward her.

"Without her I wouldn't be able to get there in time," Paul said, pulling Brown Beauty's saddle tight. "Now we have to start riding because the King's soldiers are heading this way. I have to arrive in Lexington before they do. John Hancock and Samuel Adams must be warned. Let's go!"

"Godspeed, Paul. We will follow behind, helping to spread the alarm," I said, watching Paul mount his horse and race off.

I turned around to see Liberty's jaw hanging open wide. "Are you okay?" I asked, snapping my fingers multiple times in front of his face.

"Huh? Oh, I'm more than okay, I'm F-I-N-E, fine! And speaking of fine, did you see Paul Revere's horse? Dreamy." Liberty was obviously bitten by the love bug.

"Oh, geez . . . !" Cam said, rolling his eyes.

"Liberty, focus, I need you to focus!" I said, clapping my hands by Liberty's ear. "Hurry, we have to chase after Paul Revere, he can't get too far ahead! There are too many of us to ride on Liberty, so we need another horse! Where can we find a horse in the middle of the night?"

Liberty's nose twitched as he sniffed the air. "I sense a horse near that yard over there."

"He's right," Tommy said, almost a little too loud. "I see it, right there!" Tommy pointed to a field surrounded by a wooden fence. Under the moonlight, only twenty yards away, stood a very short, pudgy pony. His light blond mane was choppy like a bad haircut and his hooves looked too big for his legs. Even from this distance, the pony stared at us like a puppy that wanted to play.

"Ah, what luck! We'll borrow the pony and return him later," I said.

"Are you kidding me?" said Cam. "No, no, no, no, no. I've had stuffed animals bigger than that thing. This is not going to work."

"I second that, for the horse record! Just saying." Liberty exclaimed.

"There's a horse record?" Tommy said, distracted by Liberty's commentary.

"Do not be fooled by appearances," I said, trying to be reassuring. "That pony may not be as fast as a horse, but I'd hang on tight if I were you. Hurry," I urged. "We don't want to miss our opportunity to ride with Paul Revere."

Cam moaned as Tommy ran over to the fence. Cam, Liberty, and I followed as Tommy quickly dislodged two of the wooden slats and led the pony out of the field and onto the dirt road. It looked like Cam was taller than the pony.

"You're killing me," said Cam, sighing.

The small pony trotted over to Liberty and looked straight up, like a little brother idolizing his big brother.

Liberty rolled his eyes and said, "Wonderful, I have a sidekick."

Tommy smiled and said, "Hey, standing side by side the two of you could be like Batman and Robin."

Liberty gave a courtesy laugh. "Ha, ha. Except Robin didn't drool and he wore a cool mask. Seriously, I think that *thing* would look better with a mask."

"What are you talking about; he kind of looks like you, Liberty," Tommy teased. "Just a little smaller. Maybe we should call him Little Liberty?"

Cam doubled over laughing, pointing at Liberty. "Oh man, he got you, Liberty."

"He looks nothing like me. I take offense to that," Liberty said, casually glancing at Little Liberty.

Little Liberty looked up with great affection at his new, *big brother*.

"All right, you three and Little Liberty. Come on, we need to hurry and catch up to Paul Revere and Brown Beauty!" I said, amused by Liberty's obvious annoyance.

"Now you're talking! That filly is my kind of lady!" Liberty said, the lovesick twinkle returning to his eyes.

"Go ahead, Mr. Revere," said Tommy. "We'll catch up."

"Yeah, we should be there in a couple hundred years," Cam moaned again.

Reluctantly, I agreed. "All right, but we won't go too far ahead. I'll be looking back often! If we ever get separated remember the code word 'Hancock-Clarke House.' That's our meeting place in Lexington."

This is the Hancock-Clarke House in modern times. Here,
Paul Revere warned John Hancock and Samuel Adams that
the Regular soldiers were coming to arrest them.

"Wait, what?" Cam asked.

"I got it," Tommy confirmed. "The Hanclarke-Lock House in Coxington. Kidding, just kidding." Tommy smiled, the usual jokester. "The Hancock-Clarke House in Lexington. I have it, really."

I smiled, relieved. "Good luck," I said. I was nervous for the boys but knew we wouldn't be far behind. "Liberty, can you do something to encourage the pony and make sure he follows toward Lexington?"

Liberty neighed at Little Liberty and stamped his left hoof three times.

Little Liberty neighed back and nodded his head.

"I get the vibe he takes these roads a lot with his owner. He seems to know exactly where he's going," said Liberty.

"All right, then. Let's go."

I waved at the boys and then turned northward as Liberty started off after Paul Revere and Brown Beauty.

Cam called out, "It can't be any worse than getting inoculated for smallpox!" his words trailing off into the distance.

I reassured myself they would be fine. Up ahead dark shadows filled the road. The night air was crisp and cold as we raced along.

"I'm sure Brown Beauty is fast but you're rocket-fast tonight," I said.

Liberty panted deeply, "Remember . . . I'm not . . . an ordinary . . . horse."

That's true, I thought. Liberty was anything but ordinary. The trees went by in a blur and the fields in blotches of blackness. It felt a little like riding the roller coaster Space Mountain at Disneyland.

* * *

Hancock-Clarke House

Concord Bridge

Buckman Tavern

Lexington Green

Paul Revere Capture Site

Paul Revere's

N
W
E
S
Paul Revere
Rush Revere
ritish Patrols
Tommy & Cam
Charles River
Ride
Old North
Church
Boston

It was around midnight when we saw Paul Revere and Brown Beauty again. They had slowed in front of a small house along the road. A man about my age listened intently as Paul warned, "Hear ye, the Regulars are coming out! They travel up the road from Boston! Let everyone know, protect yourselves!" Immediately, Paul raced off into the dead of night.

The man yelled back, "We thank you, we'll be ready! I will spread the word and we will send more riders to alarm the other towns."

The man raced back into his house. Through the window I could see him take his musket off the wall as his wife tried to comfort their crying baby. I was amazed by the response of this colonist. I knew there was more than one rider, but I did not know that riders fanned out from every village. Incredible!

"What are we waiting for?" asked Liberty. "Brown Beauty, er, I mean Paul Revere is getting away."

I turned around in the saddle and looked back to see if I could spot Cam and Tommy. Amazingly, Little Liberty was plodding along. He was only back a few hundred yards, pushing as fast as his little legs could go with Tommy and Cam gently bumping up and down.

"Let's go, Liberty," I said. We quickly resumed the chase into the middle of the night.

Every so often the moon would peek out from behind the tall trees, the thin moon rays giving off just enough light to help us see the rough outline of the surrounding countryside.

As we raced along, village after village showed similar signs of being warned by Paul Revere. Bells rang and people were awake and quickly moving around. I was just about to ask Liberty if he knew how far we were from Paul Revere when I saw a faint image of a rider up ahead.

"Liberty, that must be them, just up ahead," I said, leaning over Liberty's neck. "Hurry, let's catch up!"

As we got closer, we saw that Paul Revere and Brown Beauty had come to a stop and were waiting under the cover of a tree. "Rush, we have to go north, a different route than we intended," Paul said, pointing in the opposite direction. "We will lose a little time but rumor is there are Redcoats up ahead patrolling the roadway."

I pulled out a map to find out where we were. "Will we go up this way through Mystic?" I asked, pointing to the area on the map. It was hard to see the route in the light but Paul confirmed, "Yes, we will go through Mystic, over the wooden bridge."

Just then I heard the sound of horse hooves getting closer. I turned back to see Little Liberty still in the distance but running as fast as his little legs could take him. It was quite the sight to see the boys' heads bouncing up and down, trying to hold on.

"Oh great, the runt returns," sighed Liberty, grunting under his breath.

"Let's carry on! Onward, north towards Lexington," Paul said, starting to ride off ahead.

"We will be right behind you!" I said.

We rode through village after village and heard shouts of "Redcoats coming!" and "Hurry up!" Bells were ringing all the way until we galloped over a small rising hill into the outskirts of Lexington.

"We're almost there," Paul Revere said. "The Hancock-Clarke House is just up ahead and we can warn Hancock and Adams."

Liberty slowed to a trot as we approached a local tavern on the right with a bright red door. The sign overhead read BUCKMAN TAVERN. "Let's wait here for the boys. They will be here soon," I said, my heart racing from the excitement. A small lantern glowed in the window and a few voices could be heard inside talking and laughing. To the left was a large field about the size of a small city park. Ah, this must be Lexington Green, I thought. Several houses surrounded the field.

It seemed like years, but it was only a matter of minutes until Little Liberty trotted along to the tavern. I was glad to see the boys were still on his back. It didn't take us long to catch up to them and take the lead again. "Follow us, boys, we are very close now," I said.

"You do realize this is completely ruining my horse mojo, right? I mean, the runt is rather embarrassing. Tell me you disagree?" Liberty said in a huff. I ignored him to focus on the task at hand.

We rounded another bend and saw Paul Revere and Brown Beauty stopped in front of a two-story wooden house lined with big trees. The house was dark except for the flicker of a lamplight. A guard stood outside with a rifle on his chest.

"Just stop right there," the guard said in a loud whisper. "Don't move a step closer if ya know what's good for ya." He stood right in front of the door like it was the entrance to a treasure room.

"But I need to alarm Hancock and Adams," Paul Revere urged, spreading his chest wide. He looked about ready to explode.

"Quiet down immediately, sir, I warn you, so help me," the guard said menacingly. "Quiet down. You are about to wake the

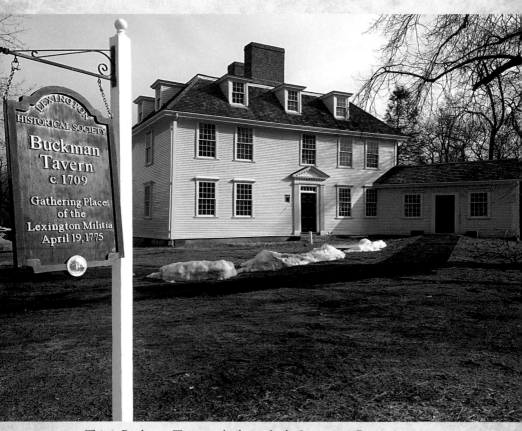

This is Buckman Tavern, which overlooks Lexington Green. American Patriots gathered here before the Battle of Lexington Green.

house with all this noise!" Brown Beauty, sweaty from head to hoof, sidestepped nervously, nostrils flaring.

"Noise?" Paul responded in his loudest voice. "Noise? You'll have noise enough before long! The Regulars are coming out!"

At that the guard's eyes widened, then he turned and immediately knocked loudly on the door, again and again.

A bedroom curtain jerked open. Then another and another. Several shadowed faces peered out into the darkness. Within a matter of seconds a man came to the door. He was dressed like he was going to a grand ball or an eighteenth-century Academy Awards show.

The man said, "Paul Revere, what is going on?" His eyes were half closed and his hair was disheveled. But he had a way about him, a surprising casualness. This wasn't Samuel Adams. The last time we saw Adams he was throwing tea into the water at Boston Harbor. Oh, of course, this must be John Hancock!

After asking Liberty to keep a lookout outside, we all pushed inside to the narrow hallway, where a candle flickered. Paul responded, "You are in grave danger, sir. The Redcoats have crossed the Charles River and are coming to get you and Sam Adams." John Hancock turned and looked at me in the eyes. He appeared surprised but quickly recovered, nodded to me, and led us farther into the house.

Samuel Adams was standing in the middle of the room with his hands on his hips. He looked grumpy.

Paul Revere introduced us to the others and said, "This is fellow Patriot Rush Revere and his two students, Tommy and Cam."

"Well, speak, Paul, we don't have all night. What is this? Something about the Redcoats coming tonight? You're joking! This is madness," said Samuel.

Cam jumped up with boldness and said, "He's not joking . . . Paul Revere is telling the truth!"

Samuel grabbed Cam by the shoulders and said, "Now this is a brave young man; finally someone answered my blessed question!" Samuel actually smiled looking at Cam, who looked at me confused.

John Hancock was casually leaning against a book cabinet. He laughed and raised a hand gently to say, "Well, we must be very, very special indeed, for all those soldiers to come after the two of us on this fine evening."

Samuel shouted, "It's no laughing matter, Hancock, the Revolution is beginning! We have to get moving right away!"

Paul looked at the others and said, "Dr. Warren thinks they plan to capture you, then move on to Concord and take the gunpowder and ammunition stores. Gunpowder is something we need, and can't produce here. Without it, we are doomed to fail. General Gage knows this; he is sending the King's soldiers to take the ammunition or worse."

"Yes, it makes sense. They are marching to Concord to snuff out any remaining freedom we still have," said John Hancock.

"Then we must warn Concord right away!" exclaimed Samuel.

John sighed. "And I suppose we will need to leave in the middle of the night. Gentlemen," he said, "I am a Patriot through and through, but I am also a man who needs a cup of tea before rising and leaving at this hour."

Tommy whispered, "Hey, Cam, what is up with this guy?"

"I know, right? He's not exactly racing to get going. C'mon, dude, they are going to hang you," Cam responded.

I pulled the boys aside while the others talked. "Don't underestimate John Hancock," I told them. "He is an incredible businessman and one of the wealthiest men in Boston. He is risking all he has for the cause. His way may be a little different, but he is a Patriot and would share that fact with King George himself."

Samuel Adams continued arguing for us to leave immediately, until John held up a relaxed finger and silenced him. "Gentlemen! Patience is a virtue. Now, if you will excuse me."

As John Hancock exited the room, Samuel Adams rolled his eyes and huffed, "Mr. Hancock is brilliant and a true Patriot, but there are times like this that I am ready to dump him in the Charles River!"

Paul Revere glanced out one of the windows and said, "It is time to go, but I don't see Dawes. I am afraid he was captured. We knew the risks of this mission, that there is a real chance we wouldn't complete it. At any point we could be captured, and God knows what the Regulars would do to us. But it is a sacrifice we are willing to make. Still, I worry about him."

"What about your family," Cam asked. "Do you have any children?"

"I can tell you this," Paul said softly, putting his hand on Cam's shoulder, "I do what I do because of my family. I want my children to live in a free country. I want them to have a choice to become anything they want to become and believe in God. I do not want a king or a government to control them."

Cam furrowed his brow and said, "You know there's a chance your kids don't understand why you're not around, right?"

"I do, but I am doing this for them. They may not understand, but I am fighting for their futures, for their freedom."

Cam looked up at Paul with soft eyes.

"Something's happening outside," Tommy said.

"It's Dawes!" Paul said, relieved. "He made it across Boston Neck!"

We all rushed outside to meet William Dawes and prepare for our next journey—to warn Concord.

As we walked down the steps I saw Liberty looking deep into Brown Beauty's eyes. Liberty seemed very happy and completely in his own world! Now I understood why he didn't give me a usual sarcastic comment when I asked him to wait outside. He was eager to make a friend!

"We need someone to stay here and be a lookout while Hancock and Adams get ready." Paul said looking at the group.

"I'll do it! I'm on it!" Tommy exclaimed.

I was torn. I didn't want to leave him alone but knew this could be a once-in-a-lifetime learning experience for him. Reluctantly I said, "Tommy, you can stay here so long as you don't leave the Hancock-Clarke House. British soldiers are patrolling the roads tonight. It is too dangerous to be out and about. I am very serious," I said nervously.

"Yep, got it. One hundred percent. I will stay right here. I'll be the lookout commando from the window! I'm good at this. I play it all the time in my backyard fort." Tommy was pumped up like he was about to start in a football game.

"What am I going to do, Mr. Revere?" Cam asked.

"I want you to come to Concord with Paul Revere and me," I replied.

"Am I riding on Little Liberty?" Cam eagerly continued. Liberty looked away from his conversation with Brown Beauty for a second to glare my way and shake his head.

"No, this time you can ride on Liberty with me," I said.

"Whew," Cam said, "I'm moving up from coach to first class!"

I am sure Liberty was desperate to say something but he restrained himself.

"Okay, Cam, let's go say goodbye to Samuel Adams and John Hancock," I said.

Paul Revere and Brown Beauty, Dawes and his sturdy mare, and Cam, Liberty, and I left Lexington and headed west to Concord. We were on the road only for a couple of miles when we were overtaken by another man on a horse. He was a handsome young gentleman, richly dressed, and mounted on an impressive stallion.

The man rode up between us and said, "Good evening, sirs." He glanced at his pocket watch. "Or, I guess I should say good morning since it's nearly one o'clock. My name is Dr. Samuel Prescott. I heard from some people down the road that you are headed to Concord, to warn them to hide the town's gunpowder and weapons."

"And what are you doing out at one o'clock in the morning?" Paul asked, suspicious.

He went on to interrogate Dr. Prescott for a bit and found him to be a true Patriot. We also found out he was visiting his fiancée and was originally from Concord. Dr. Prescott's knowledge of the town would likely come in handy.

We rode into the early morning. Despite the late hour, Cam was wide awake and full of energy.

Suddenly, we heard Paul Revere shout, "Regulars!"

"Where?" shouted Dawes, pulling hard on his horse. Prescott turned his horse sideways skillfully.

Paul warned, "There are Regular soldiers on horses lurking up ahead, under that tree. It's an ambush!"

"What should we do?" I asked.

"I propose we attack," urged Paul boldly. "Are you with me?"

The other men instantly agreed and without further discussion we raced forward.

The moonlight shone brightly and the tall trees near the road created ghostly moon shadows. The road curved up ahead, and beyond the bend there were even more British soldiers on horseback.

One of the British soldiers shouted, "Stop! If you go an inch farther you are dead!"

We had no chance to fight them. We were outnumbered.

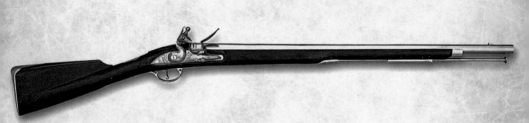

A rifle similar to this was used during
the American Revolution. Careful, Rush Revere!

Chapter 5

*T*he *British soldiers* completely blocked the road now, and there was no way through. "You there, *stop*! Any further and you are a dead man!" shouted a tall British Redcoat pointing his pistol in our direction. The British soldiers wore full dress uniforms with swords and pistols in their hands. They had positioned their horses to block, but Brown Beauty and Paul Revere raced forward into them. The road narrowed where the Redcoats waited. It was the perfect spot to prevent us from passing.

Liberty slowed and asked, "What's our plan, Captain?"

I replied, "I'm not exactly sure what happens next, but—"

"Wait, what?" interrupted Liberty. "You're supposed to be the history expert. What do you mean you're not sure?"

"I'm thinking I should've stayed back with Tommy," Cam said.

The British soldiers were all around us.

Liberty and Brown Beauty whinnied and whirled as if they were standing in a pit of vipers.

"I don't think we are going to get out of this one, Mr. Revere," Cam said in a panic, searching desperately for a way out.

Suddenly, Dr. Prescott shouted, "Put on!"

I guess that is Yankee language for "get going" because the next second, Dr. Prescott and his stallion sprinted left toward a low stone wall. Paul Revere and Brown Beauty sprinted right toward a grove of trees at the far end of the pasture. And William Dawes and his horse darted in a third direction, toward a nearby farm.

"Hang on, Cam!" I yelled, urging Liberty forward.

Liberty joined Brown Beauty as both horses shot off across the moonlit pasture like cats running from firecrackers.

"Do you see Dr. Prescott or William Dawes? Did they escape?" I yelled to Cam, who was holding on tight.

"I think so," Cam replied, breathing heavy. "That doctor dude and his horse jumped superhigh over that huge stone wall and the British couldn't do it."

Paul Revere rode a few feet in front of us. We made it through the undergrowth and lunged into the tree line of the nearby woods. Wet ice and mud flew up under Liberty's hooves. Suddenly he slowed.

"It's a trap," warned Liberty, breathing hard.

"What do you mean?" I asked.

"I'm not sure," Liberty panted. "This doesn't feel right."

In a flash, six Redcoats appeared from among the trees. Their horses prodded the ground and snorted as if they were revving their engines. Ten of them now surrounded us.

Paul Revere and Brown Beauty came to a halt and we stopped right beside them.

"Get off your horses, or we'll blow your brains out!" yelled an officer. He scowled and pointed his pistol at Paul's head and grabbed Brown Beauty. Another pointed his gun at my head. It was so close I could see down the barrel.

Cam slipped off the back of Liberty and I dismounted, too. The Redcoats didn't wait for Paul to dismount. Instead, they yanked him from his saddle and pulled him to the ground. A Redcoat kicked him in the ribs. Paul grunted as another boot kicked him from the other side.

Cam started forward to help, but I held him back. "Let me go, Mr. Revere, we need to stop this, they are hurting Paul!"

I didn't know what to do. Luckily I didn't have to intervene. The British commanding officer quickly shouted, "Leave him! We are not savages. Put this gentleman with the others."

Two Redcoats lifted Paul by his arms. Everything was dark around us. Paul cringed as they touched him. His face and clothes were drenched with mud and ice. The Redcoats pulled and dragged him over to where Cam and I stood with . . .

I searched left and right. "Where's Liberty?" I softly asked Cam.

He looked just as surprised as I was. "He must have held his breath and disappeared when we were watching the Redcoats grab Paul Revere," said Cam.

The commanding British officer approached Paul and asked in a gruff voice, "What is your name?"

Paul Revere stood tall and squared his shoulders to the officer. With a penetrating stare he replied with authority, "My name is Revere!"

"What?" asked the officer, taking a step backward. "Paul Revere! *The* Paul Revere?" His look of surprise turned into jubilation, as if he had just caught the most wanted man in New England.

"Yes," replied Paul. For a split second I thought I saw a slight grin on Paul's face.

The Redcoats heaped abuse on him. "Rebel, rabble-rouser, scoundrel, traitor!" they yelled and moved closer as if to strike him.

Cam shook his head and said, "These guys really hate him, don't they?"

I nodded.

The British commander drilled Paul with questions just inches from his face. One after the other. "Are you an express rider? What message do you carry? Where were you headed?"

"I am happy to answer your questions," said Paul. "Yes, I am an express rider."

"And what message do you bring?" the British commander asked.

"One that is no secret to you," said Paul Revere. He raised his voice and with boldness and energy replied, "Gentlemen, Hancock and Adams have already been warned. They are long gone. You've missed your aim."

"What of our aim?" the officer said. "We are simply looking for deserters."

Paul gave a knowing smile. "And I'm just a silversmith selling my spoons and teapots in the middle of the night."

"What's Paul doing?" whispered Cam.

"He's being very clever, turning the interrogation around," I said. "He's telling them that the cat is out of the bag. He's trying to let them know that the surprise is lost."

"Oh, that is genius!" exclaimed Cam.

This is the site of Paul Revere's capture by the King's soldiers on his famous Midnight Ride. Scary!

Paul stared at each of them and said, "I know better. I know what you are after and have alarmed the country all the way up from Boston."

The British commanding officer was becoming more enraged by the second and clapped his pistol to Paul Revere's head. "If you do not tell the truth, I am going to take this gun and blow your brains out." The officer gave a wicked smile.

Paul glared at the man and said serenely, "I do not need a threat to make me speak the truth. I call myself a man of truth, and you have stopped me on a highway, and made me a prisoner I know not of what right. I will tell the truth, for I am not afraid." A smile crept across Paul's face as he revealed the secret plans of his enemy. "In the dead of night a column of troops left Boston by boat and crossed the Back Bay, and came across at Cambridge."

"Nonsense!" shouted the commander. But the men began to whisper to each other nervously.

"If you value your lives I would stay far away from Lexington. I expect five hundred men there soon," Paul said.

Clearly, Paul Revere was trying to lead the British away from Hancock and Adams in Lexington.

A chubby British Redcoat jumped when an owl hooted from a nearby tree.

The British commander's eyes fell upon Cam. He reached out his hand and lifted Cam's chin until he was staring into his eyes. "Do you want to be let go, boy?" he asked. "Tell your friend to give us the answers we need." Cam bit his teeth together and stared directly into the Redcoat's eyes.

The commander pushed Cam away. "You little fool," he exclaimed. He raised his pistol and pointed it at Paul Revere.

All of a sudden, out of nowhere, a single gunshot ripped through the dark and quiet night air. My heart leapt. I pulled Cam back away from the noise and under my arm. I couldn't bring myself to look. Did he really just shoot Paul Revere? Heaven help us, we have changed history, I thought. We killed Paul Revere. I forced myself to look back at Paul's body and found him still standing.

The British commander jerked his head around and asked, "What was that?"

Whew! I breathed a sigh of relief. Paul Revere was not shot. The sound had come from somewhere in the distance, from Lexington.

"I told you," said Paul with a slight grin. "The colony of Massachusetts has been warned. Lexington is ready to fight. You will all be rounded up and put in prison for life. And the country folk are not exactly happy with what you have done to them."

Suddenly the sky erupted with a thunderous explosion of musket fire. An entire volley of gunshots echoed through the trees and pasture. It sounded like loud firecrackers all going off at the same time. The soldier's horses bucked and skidded backward as the Redcoats pulled at their reins.

"They are shooting at Lexington. Paul Revere speaks the truth," said a Redcoat.

"Like I said, I am a man of truth," Paul repeated.

Finally, we could hear the distant sound of Lexington's town bell ringing wildly.

"Can you hear that?" exclaimed Paul. "The people of Lexington and all the towns within the sound of those bells know you are here. As I said before, your surprise is lost."

A look of horror appeared on the British commander's face.

Brilliant! I thought. Even at the peril of his own life, Paul Revere delayed ten British soldiers and tricked them into thinking that they were known to the American Patriots in Lexington.

"Bring me the prisoners' horses," barked the British commander.

Brown Beauty was held by a nearby Redcoat. The other officers quickly scanned the area but found no sign of Liberty. The commander glared at me and asked, "Where in blazes is your horse?"

"Honestly, I don't know," I said.

"You are all liars. No matter, you won't be needing it," he said. "You may keep your life, Paul Revere. But I will keep your horse. It is a fine specimen—one worthy of a commander in the British army, don't you think?" The commander smirked and walked over to Brown Beauty and hoisted himself onto the saddle. He slapped her hard on the neck and she stepped back.

"On your horses, men!" he ordered the other Redcoats.

"Liberty will be devastated," I said. He had an obvious crush on Brown Beauty from the moment he saw her.

The British commander kicked his spurs into Brown Beauty's stomach. She recoiled and pulled backward. "Curse you and your Patriot spies," exclaimed the commander.

The ten soldiers spurred their horses down the path. As they moved out, several spit at us and one shouted, "Bloody rebels!"

Paul Revere let out a breath of air and said, "Well, we fooled them, didn't we?"

"Are you okay?" I asked.

"I am, but now we need to get back to Lexington one way or another. We may not have our horses, but we still have our lives and our freedom," Paul said, grabbing his shoulder and wiping some of the dirt and blood off his jacket.

"How did you stay so calm? I mean it was crazy. Those guys wanted to kill you and you sounded totally casual like it happens every day," Cam said. He looked at Paul with large eyes.

"It is important to never let your opponent know your true feelings. I was nervous on the inside but I knew if I showed that on my face, it would have been a different ending," Paul said. "You were very brave yourself. You are a great example of a young Patriot. You make us proud. Your father must be a very brave man to have raised a son with so much courage."

You could see Cam stand up taller as he thought about the compliment.

"We must hurry on. It is inevitable now. The war is about to begin and we have much work to do," Paul said and started to walk ahead.

Under the bright moonlight, we watched the Redcoats ride away. My heart sank as I realized how badly they would treat Brown Beauty. Just as they started to fade in the distance one British rider flew backward off his horse and fell to the ground.

"Did you see that?" Cam asked, flabbergasted.

I nodded, equally surprised. "It looked like a branch of a tree had snapped backward and knocked the rider off the horse. It was as if someone had pulled back the branch as far as it could go and then let it whip forward at just the right moment."

We kept watching closely as Brown Beauty kicked up her back legs in celebration and raced away under the moonlight. The British commander jumped on his original horse and they all galloped away.

Cam whispered, "Mr. Revere, I think Liberty just rescued Brown Beauty."

"No doubt," I replied softly. "There's a hero in all of us. And it typically comes out when we're fighting to free ourselves or those we love."

"Unless one of our horses comes back soon it looks like we'll be walking back to Lexington!" said Paul Revere.

"With all the gunfire in Lexington I'm pretty worried about Tommy," I said.

"I can understand your concern," said Paul Revere. "The collective shot we heard earlier sounded like the Lexington Patriots clearing their muskets. If we hurry we can get there before the King's army arrives."

A flash of movement caught our eye. We turned and saw Liberty galloping in our direction. He was alone. What happened to Brown Beauty, I thought?

"Liberty!" Cam shouted.

Liberty slowed to a trot and then walked right up to us.

"You have a very smart horse," said Paul, reaching out to pat Liberty's neck.

"Yes," I said, and mumbled, "you don't know the half of it."

I must admit I was thrilled to see Liberty. I whispered in his ear, "Where is Brown Beauty?" He shrugged his shoulders as if to suggest he didn't know. There had to be more to that story but it wasn't the time to ask.

Paul Revere picked up his pace and said, "There is a trunk at the Buckman Tavern with secret papers from John Hancock that must be moved. I need to go and secure those. I know a shortcut back to town. I recommend you ride your horse to the

Hancock-Clarke House and check on Tommy. Take the main road. With the bells still ringing you should be safe."

"Thank you," I said sincerely. "Godspeed, Paul Revere."

Paul gave us a warm smile before he left down the road toward Lexington. "Be safe, fellow Sons of Liberty, our cause is glorious!"

I quickly hoisted myself up onto Liberty and Cam joined me. Liberty turned and began a fast trot down the main road.

Our return trip to Lexington took longer than I remembered. And it felt darker and colder, too. The moon had already dipped below some tall oak and beech trees. All we could see was the lamplights of distant homesteads, and all we could hear was the sound of distant bells. Cam was getting tired. I think the excitement kept him awake much longer than normal but as we rode he leaned against my back, half asleep. I was feeling the effects of the late night and the capture, too, but I knew we had to go on. Even Liberty was oddly quiet. The only thing he said about Brown Beauty as we left the pasture was that he hoped those soldiers didn't capture her again. I'm sure her well-being consumed his thoughts. As the wind gently blew through the trees and branches, bits of ice fell onto my coat and Liberty's mane.

"I am starting to think I made a huge mistake leaving Tommy back in Lexington," I told Liberty. "I got caught up in the moment with Hancock and Adams and thought it would be a great learning experience. But I fear I may have put him at risk. I shouldn't have left him there."

"If it makes you feel any better, Lexington is right around this bend," said Liberty.

The sun was still below the horizon but its rays pushed up

and over the low hills and countryside. As we rounded the bend, I still couldn't see any buildings, but I could clearly hear the Lexington bell. The sound was loud enough to wake up Cam.

"Those bells make a great alarm clock," he said groggily.

"Indeed," I said, "it looks like Dr. Warren's plan has worked. The bells are ringing all over the countryside."

Sleepily, Cam said, "Just like the Pilgrims' bell." He yawned. "Tommy told me how the Pilgrims used a bell to warn them of danger, too."

What an interesting thought. I loved how these children remembered everything.

As we entered the city, I was alarmed to see hundreds of British Redcoats standing in formation near the center of town, muskets in hand and ready to fight. "Liberty, take us behind that church," I said, hoping it would keep us out of the line of fire. The white church steeple rose above Lexington Green. The green was a large field and Cam, Liberty, and I stood at the far end from where the Redcoats stood. I glanced at my watch and was surprised to see it was nearly five o'clock in the morning.

"Why are all those people standing around in front?" Cam asked.

"They are blocking the road to Concord," I replied.

There were not many American soldiers, perhaps seventy. None of them were wearing uniforms. They looked like farmers. One was wearing work clothes and carried an old rifle; another wore a blue hat that nearly covered his face. Many wore knee-length breeches. None stood in formation. I could not imagine how this group could take on the soldiers of the mighty British Empire.

Suddenly a single gunshot rang out straight ahead. Liberty jolted backward.

This is Lexington Green in modern times. Look how close the houses are to the battle site. They were there in 1775.

As we peered around the corner of the church, gunfire rippled through the air and a look of pure chaos filled the streets near the Buckman Tavern. A cloud of white smoke rose in front of a couple hundred Regulars. Had these British troops fired their muskets at the Lexington Patriots? It felt like the Boston Massacre all over again.

The Americans ran in all directions toward the safety of the buildings that surrounded the Green, and where women and children watched from their porches. A woman in the doorway of a house to our left began to scream.

Scattered gunfire continued as more and more Regulars shot their muskets. It sounded like the sky had cracked open as lead balls ripped through anything in their path. Frightened horses bolted forward searching for refuge. Clouds of dirty musket smoke filled the air and made it difficult to see what was happening.

Suddenly, Cam pointed and shouted, "Look! By that house! There's a kid on the porch right in the middle of the battle! He's going to get shot!"

Where is he pointing, I thought? I couldn't see the kid he was referring to.

"Oh, no, Tommy???" Cam shouted.

My heart sank just like it had when Brown Beauty was taken from Paul Revere. I looked closer to where Cam was pointing. Sure enough, amid the scattering spectators was a blond-haired boy who looked about the size of Tommy. He was standing near a house about a hundred yards from the Buckman Tavern. The British Redcoats were only a house or two away. A woman stood right behind him holding his shoulder.

"What on earth is Tommy doing there?" I shouted in a panic

over the noise. I was truly terrified, like someone had just snuck up behind me in a dark room.

"Tommy!" Cam yelled, waving his hands above his head like a drowning swimmer.

"Cam, get down, they are shooting!"

"Should I go get him?" Liberty said in a serious tone.

"Tommy! Tommy!" Cam kept screaming over and over but the shouting, screams, and gunfire were too deafening. "Mr. Revere, we can't let anything happen to him. He's my best friend." Desperately, Cam called out one more time as loud as his lungs allowed him. "Tommy!"

Tommy finally heard his name being shouted and looked our way. It was hard to feel angry at him for disobeying me because all I really wanted was for him to get to a safe place.

Tommy shouted back, "Little Liberty is in that stable, we have to save him!" He slipped out of the woman's grasp and ran through the Green toward a small stable.

"Cam stay here with Liberty. Do not move, do you hear me?" I said frantically.

All of a sudden I realized that we were watching the Battle of Lexington Green.

The historian in me was thrilled to see the battle I had read about over and over again. But the teacher in me was panic-stricken. "Tommy!" I yelled. "Get out of there! Run!" I couldn't believe what I had done . . . why did I leave him?

Tommy ran behind a large tree and used it as a shield. Tree bark splintered violently as a lead ball hit the large trunk.

"We need to get him out of there," Cam shouted, and made a move to chase Tommy, but I held him back.

"Cam, those are real bullets and we are in real danger, stay down," I said, but I couldn't take my own advice. I ducked down and started running toward the tree, the bullets, the smoke, and toward the people fleeing the Redcoats. I could barely see. My eyes burned from the gunpowder and the air smelled like burnt matches.

I didn't get far because Tommy was on the move again. He bolted from the tree and dashed to the nearby stable. I was about to follow him when the sound of a lead ball whizzed by my ear. I fell flat on my stomach, heart pounding.

I lifted my head and yelled, "Tommy, get down, get down!" Over and over I screamed above the sounds of the battle. Bits of cloth were below my feet. Shouts seemed to come from all around. I could barely make out the Buckman Tavern in front of me. It all seemed to go in slow motion as I pushed forward toward Tommy.

"Mr. Revere, I have to save Little Liberty!" Tommy yelled as he reached the edge of the stable.

I could see the stable was on fire. Tommy climbed through a fence and started opening the horse stalls. Like a jailbreak, the horses ran for freedom. But there was one stall still closed. Tommy raced forward on his hands and knees, trying to keep low. As Tommy lifted the latch, the stall door sprung open and Little Liberty bounded out the door like a playful puppy. The pony looked oblivious to the battle.

Tommy hopped onto the back of Little Liberty and nudged the pony forward. Together they raced out of the burning stable and toward the white church. The Redcoats were reloading their muskets.

Bang! A shot fired from a musket to my left. I was close

enough to see the puff of smoke lift from the gun. Suddenly the smoke stopped in midair. The Redcoat holding the musket stood like a statue in a wax museum. The British army, the Lexington Patriots, the spectators, the horses, and even Tommy's pony had frozen in time. It looked like a giant game of freeze tag and everyone had been tagged except Tommy. He sat on top of Little Liberty, who was stopped in mid-gallop, his tongue halfway out of his mouth like he'd licked an icy pole.

"What just happened?" Cam asked.

"We don't have much time, literally!" said Liberty as we all rushed toward Tommy. "I can hold off time only until I blink again," he warned.

Within seconds we were at Tommy's side. Inches from his back was a lead ball suspended in the air.

"Whew! Am I glad to see you guys!" said Tommy, caught up in the moment.

Cam reached out to grab the lead ball but he couldn't pull it from its midair flight.

"It's stuck," Cam said. "It won't move an inch."

"That's because it's frozen in time," Liberty said quickly.

I clarified: "As soon as Liberty blinks everything will continue on its course through time. We're not from this time period so we're not affected by Liberty's time control."

"Enough talking, just save Tommy!" Liberty shouted. "I can't hold this much longer."

"Tommy, jump on Liberty's back!" I shouted.

"No, I'm not leaving Little Liberty," exclaimed Tommy.

"Then lean over to your left," I said, tugging on his shirt. "Can you see the trajectory of the lead ball?"

"Eyes burning . . . can't hold . . . gonna blink!" warned Liberty.

Tommy turned his head and glanced at the lead ball and then looked over at the Regular who shot it. "Yeah, I see it."

"Good!" I shouted. "Just lean like that and you'll be fine. When time starts again, race to the church!"

Suddenly the world exploded in surround sound.

As Little Liberty bounced forward the momentum raised Tommy a little higher. I had not taken that into consideration, and the lead ball ripped through the side of Tommy's coat sleeve.

Tommy grimaced and gritted his teeth as Little Liberty and Big Liberty raced side by side until we found ourselves sheltered behind the church again.

A look of disbelief was on Tommy's face. "I think I was shot," he said, wincing in pain. "But at least Little Liberty's safe."

I quickly examined the wound. "It only grazed the skin. You are extremely lucky, Tommy, you could have been really hurt or worse," I said. "It is unacceptable that you didn't do as I told you. You were supposed to stay with Hancock and Adams, away from the battle at the Hancock-Clarke House. What were you thinking?"

"I wasn't, Mr. Revere. I am so sorry," Tommy said with his head down.

"Tommy, you almost made me wet my pants. You gotta be more careful," Cam said while shaking his head.

"It's just that when you guys didn't come back I thought you had been captured and I got worried. I guess I forgot about our agreement and followed some of the neighbors to the loud sounds."

"Tommy, I am angry with you right now because I care about you and your safety very much. From now on, you must listen to me, understood?"

Liberty snorted, "And so you decided to play Superman? For the record, you're not faster than a speeding bullet."

"I know, Liberty," Tommy said, his head still down. "But when the British army arrived everything got crazy. I felt like I was lost in a huge mall filled with strangers. The British were yelling and the Americans were yelling and it got really scary. Then the first gunshot rang out and everyone just started running everywhere."

"I am sorry I let this happen," I said.

Little Liberty nickered and licked Tommy's face.

"Did that pony just lick you?" said Liberty. "Seriously, someone has got to teach him proper pony etiquette."

I couldn't help but smile. "I guess you have someone who is happy you were there in his hour of need." Little Liberty was still licking Tommy's smiling face.

Tommy lowered his voice and asked, "What's up with Cam?"

I turned and noticed Cam staring out at the battlefield. His brow was furrowed, his eyes were dazed, and his lips were barely moving. He carried a deep sadness on his face.

I walked over to him and tenderly said, "Cam, I know this has been a crazy day. You were unbelievably brave. I am so proud of you." I put my hand on his shoulder.

Reverently, Cam replied, "I count at least a half dozen Lexington men lying on the ground. They're not moving."

In the distance, families and loved ones cried as they stood above their fathers, husbands, and sons. Many soldiers were badly wounded and others looked beyond help.

"Cam, war is a horrible thing. I'm sorry you had to see this kind of suffering," I said solemnly. It was one of those times when you don't have the right words, and no matter what you say, it won't make it easier.

The American Patriot soldiers were nicknamed Minutemen, among other nicknames. This is a statue of an American Minuteman at Lexington Green. Do you notice how his clothing is different from the Redcoats' clothing?

"It is time for us to go home," I said, taking Cam's arm to turn him around.

It was now dawn and the sun had peeked over the rolling hills. We were all a bit stunned and exhausted after everything we had just seen. I knew the kids needed a good meal, a warm shower, and time to think about everything they had been through. This was a day they weren't soon to forget.

After Liberty told Little Liberty he'd be back to visit him soon, the boys climbed up onto Liberty's saddle and he quietly said, *"Rush, rush, rushing from history."*

The portal opened and swirled. As we left I looked back to see Little Liberty chomping on some grass, unaware of the critical moment in history we had all just witnessed.

★ SUPPORT OUR TROOPS ★

Volunteers Needed!

We are putting together special care packages to send to our military heroes serving overseas. Please join us for a pack and ship party!

Where: Manchester Middle School Gym

When: Saturday, November 15th @ 9:00 AM

COMPLIMENTARY BBQ PICNIC AND REFRESHMENTS FOR ALL VOLUNTEERS!

For further information, please contact Danielle@MilitaryFamiliesCare.us

GOD BLESS AMERICA!

While Cam's father is in Afghanistan, Cam's mother, Danielle, and other spouses are working hard at home to support our troops. This is a flyer that was given to Rush Revere for an upcoming special event at Manchester Middle School.

Chapter 6

After our last adventure, I was relieved to be back in modern day. I wondered, though, what happened to Paul Revere. We had lost him after the Battle of Lexington. So, I looked through my history books and discovered that he made it back to Lexington and hid John Hancock's secret trunk. Phew! I was happy with the news.

As I walked across the military base toward a large green field, Cam called over to me and said, "Thanks for coming, Mr. Revere." He was standing with Tommy and Freedom at the edge of what looked like a large soccer field. The grass had been recently cut and there were spectators lined up on either side. I was wondering where they came from!

"I'm glad you invited me. I wouldn't miss it," I said as I walked across the lawn to greet them.

"Hi, Mr. Revere, is Liberty here?" Tommy asked. His eyes scanned left and right.

"No," Freedom replied for me. "I don't sense his, oh, wait, I found him." Freedom smiled. "He says he's at a horse spa recovering from his trip to Boston and Lexington."

"He's right about that," I replied a little guiltily. "Liberty did all the running and jumping. His legs were pretty tired and sore after the trip."

"Hey, losers," said Billy, who stood with about a dozen other kids about ten yards away. His hands were on his hips with his big chest out. They all wore matching red T-shirts with the words FEAR THE BILLY printed in white. Ah, yes. I remembered Billy the Bully, and I must say I was not particularly happy to see him. First a fistfight, then taunting Cam in the gym. Not a pleasant young man. I was not exactly sure but it looked like the game was dodgeball.

"Is this all you've got on your team?" Billy scoffed. "Couldn't you get any more losers to join you?"

The chubby boy named Edward, known as Ed, whom Cam had first protected ran onto the field toward Cam's team. He tripped on his shoelaces and went down, face-first. Wobbling, he pushed himself to his knees. Awkwardly he stood up and rushed over to his three teammates.

"I made it, Cam," said Ed. "Sorry I'm late. I had to finish my calculus homework."

"Hey, great, you got fatty the nerd with you, good luck," Billy taunted. The rest of the kids on Billy's team laughed.

"Looks can be deceiving, Billy. We may look like underdogs but we'll put up a fight."

Billy grabbed his stomach and laughed. "More like the under . . . pants." His team laughed again.

"Hey, Ed, glad you could make it," Cam said, not very convincingly. He searched the rest of the field for other latecomers. Nope. It looked like it would only be the four of them against the bully and his large crew. Things were not looking good.

Billy kept trash-talking as he yelled, "I hope you have a team doctor. You're gonna need one!"

Cam yelled back, "Yeah, we have a doctor, his name is Dr. Warren." Cam and Freedom started laughing quietly. Ed asked, "Did I miss something?"

Billy shouted, "Never heard of him. Must be the guy who changes your diapers." Billy laughed as if he were hilarious.

"Nope," replied Cam, "the only diaper on this field is the one you're wearing." Cam high-fived his laughing teammates.

"You won't be laughing for long," Billy said. "Look at us! We're bigger, stronger, and faster than you. And we totally have you outnumbered. Face it, you have zero chance of winning."

Cam shot back, "Oh yeah? Dr. Warren thinks we have a chance. But you can call him Dr. Doom!"

That seemed to shut Billy up.

Freedom nudged Cam and whispered, "I thought you said you invited more friends to be on our team."

"I did," Cam said in a hushed voice. "Nobody showed. I guess they were too busy."

"Or too scared," said Freedom.

"Or too smart," said Tommy.

"Hey, I'm smart," said Ed. "Anyone need help with your homework? Chemistry is my specialty. But I'm also good at bioelectronics, quantum physics, and complex—"

Tommy interrupted and said, "How about human anatomy? We'll probably need someone to reattach our limbs after the game."

If I remembered correctly from the last time I played dodge-ball as a kid, the rules were simple. You throw balls at kids on the other team, and if you hit them with the ball they are out. But if they catch the ball you throw, you are out. The game ends when all kids on one side are out.

Cam tried to reassure his teammates. "Look, I'll tell Billy that our whole team didn't show and we'll need to reschedule. It's all good."

Cam walked over to Billy, who stood nearly a head taller than him. "Hey, Billy, as you can see we're shorthanded."

"Nah, you're just short," said Billy as his fellow bullies laughed.

"I'm serious," Cam said. "We only have four players. So we're going to have to reschedule."

"Nice try, doofus," said Billy. "Just because I'm prepared and you're not doesn't mean I'm letting you forfeit! Game on!"

"No way!" Cam said firmly. "I'm all for competing against you, Billy. But winning like this doesn't prove anything."

Billy stared at Cam and smirked. "All right," he said. "We'll consider today's game a first-round game. Now everyone will get to see you lose twice. Got it?" he exclaimed as he poked his finger into Cam's shoulder blade. "If you lose this round, your team has to do twenty laps around the park, no matter how long it takes."

"Got it," Cam said. He turned around and walked across the centerline. When he returned he told his team what Billy agreed to and that this first game was only a scrimmage. The news didn't put any smiles on his teammates' faces.

Balls were lined up in the middle of the field.

"Good luck," I said, giving them a thumbs-up. I tried to hide my real feeling that this was not going to end well. I jogged to the side of the field with the other spectators. Cam ran over to me and said, "Any last-minute bit of advice coach?"

"You have a small team but you have a bigger heart. Don't forget that," I said. "Remember, win or lose, I am proud of you all."

Both teams took their positions ten yards from either side of the centerline.

"What exactly are we supposed to do? What's our objective?" Ed asked.

Before Cam could explain, a whistle sounded. Cam, Tommy, and Freedom bolted toward the center to grab a rubber ball. Billy and his team did the same thing. Ed looked on in fascination like he was watching the splitting of an atom.

It happened so fast. I'm not even sure which side threw the first ball. Suddenly a flurry of blurs darted across the centerline, mostly coming from Billy's team.

Ed was smart enough to realize that standing there was not to his advantage. He quickly ran forward and then backward and then to the left and to the right. I wasn't sure if he had to go to the bathroom or if he was warming up to do the hokey-pokey. In the end it really didn't matter because Ed never saw the melon-sized meteor hurtling toward his face. It slammed into the side of his head and sent his cheeks jiggling and his body wiggling until the vibration slowed and he finally fell backward onto a bed of grass.

Tommy and Cam had already thrown their balls and were now jumping and dodging the best they could. Freedom deflected a ball with her own and dodged another before she threw her ball at a red-shirted player. The field was just too big and Billy's team had too many players and they were too spread out.

"Fire!" yelled Billy as a volley of shots sailed over the line toward Cam, Tommy, and Freedom. The number of incoming balls was just too high. Tommy got hit in the shoulder as he tried to jump over a low-flying ball. Freedom spun sideways only to be hit by two balls coming from opposite directions. Cam somersaulted to the side and inadvertently stepped out of bounds. He was automatically disqualified.

I looked on from the sidelines. The game was over almost as soon as it began. No matter how much I hoped they would win, the odds were just too stacked against them.

"Chin up!" I yelled at the team. "You'll get 'em next time."

"Don't remind us," mumbled Cam.

"Yeah, it might be easier if we took on a herd of stampeding elephants," replied Freedom as she hobbled off the field.

Billy beat his chest like a gorilla and then pointed at the FEAR THE BILLY lettering. His team gave each other high fives and fist bumps. They towered over Cam's team. The game was over. Some of the crowd clapped and whistled.

Billy yelled over to Cam, "Time to do some laps!" Billy pointed to a teammate and said, "My friend here is going to make sure you do all twenty. I'll hear about it if you don't! See you tomorrow, losers!" He walked off the field with the rest of his gloating team.

Cam punched his hand with his fist. He was clearly frustrated.

"Look, you may have lost this battle but you haven't lost the war," I said. "Remember the Battle of Lexington? What you didn't see during your last visit was that the Americans didn't give up after their devastating loss. My advice is for you all to go home and get some rest. Tomorrow, we'll learn about the Battle of Concord. It might give you some ideas on how to beat your bully opponent."

"We don't stand a chance," Cam said. "Why even bother?"

"Because the bullies can't always win," Freedom said. "Sometimes the underdogs win. Next time that will be us."

Tommy added, "Yes, we just need to beat them at their own game. We gotta figure a way."

I chimed in, trying to cheer him up: "Don't forget what Paul Revere said. Never give up, even if the odds are stacked against you. Let's meet at Manchester Middle School tomorrow and get planning."

The three students reluctantly nodded. It was time to do some laps.

Five yards away in the grass, Ed sat up from where he was lying and groggily asked, "Did we win?"

The next morning Freedom, Cam, and Tommy arrived at Manchester Middle School at ten o'clock. They each chose desks in the front row and slumped into their chairs. Cam looked particularly discouraged.

"Good morning," I said. "Why all the sour faces?"

"Don't you remember we got spanked yesterday?" Cam asked. "It was almost as bad as watching the battle. Plus our legs are falling off from all the running."

"We just need a new plan," said Freedom positively.

"Well, you came to the right place," I said, beaming.

The sound of a desk sliding against the classroom floor got my attention. I turned to see Liberty trying to sit like the other kids and fit into a desk.

Cam and Tommy looked at each other and nearly burst out laughing.

"Liberty, you're not going to fit into that desk," I said. "It's impossible."

"Fine," Liberty harrumphed. "Then I'll just sit on top of it."

Liberty positioned his rump in front of the small desk and then lowered his back legs. Instantly, Liberty flattened the desk like a car crusher at a junkyard.

Freedom jumped out of her desk and rushed over to help Liberty. As soon as Cam and Tommy realized that Liberty wasn't hurt, they both started laughing hysterically.

"How about we all pretend that didn't happen," Liberty said, blushing.

Cam said, "Hey, Liberty, you know you're not supposed to bring food into class."

"Food?" Liberty asked, perking up. "I don't see any food."

"I do," said Cam. "That desk is as flat as a pancake!"

The boys laughed so hard they nearly fell over.

"Just ignore them, Liberty," said Freedom.

"You know what they say: what goes around comes around."

"All right, enough of this horseplay," I said. "I'm glad Liberty was able to cheer you up but we have a lot to discuss today. First things first. Yesterday's dodgeball game with Billy is in the past. Yes, you were beaten badly. But moping about it isn't going to help you win. Your friend Ed has the right idea. I understand he bounced back quickly and is studying dodgeball techniques. He's determined to come better prepared for this next game. What could *you* learn that will help you win your next battle? That's why you're here this morning. Liberty, are you ready to time-travel?"

"You bet," said Liberty. "I'm rested and ready to rumble to the Battle of Concord."

"Wait a minute," Freedom said, worried. "I thought you said we wouldn't have to time-travel."

"Yeah, won't the Battle of Concord be just as dangerous as the Battle of Lexington?" asked Tommy.

"Actually, yes," I said. "And knowing the dangers I think it's best that you stay here this morning. Liberty and I will be the only ones time-jumping."

"What are we going to do?" Freedom asked.

"Yeah, you know it's not very responsible for a teacher to leave his students without adult supervision," Cam teased.

"Oh yeah, I learned that one the hard way," Tommy said.

"I'm sorry about that again, Tommy. I shouldn't have left you. Anyway, that's the beauty of time travel," I said with a smile. "You'll barely know we've been gone since we'll return within a second or two after we've left. Liberty and I will experience first-hand the Battle of Concord and then we'll return and report the historical truth."

"And you think that truth will help us win our next dodgeball game against Billy?" Tommy asked.

I nodded. "I want you to remember this. Smart people know American history. But the really sharp ones use it for their future success. History tells us that the Americans won the Battle of Concord. But we need to ask ourselves how that was possible if the British had a bigger army and were better prepared."

"You really think we'll find a strategy to win?" Cam asked hopefully.

"It's worth a jump, don't you think?" I replied.

They all nodded and we quickly moved the desks so there

was a center aisle big enough for Liberty. I hoisted myself into Liberty's saddle and said, "Liberty, we're headed for April 19th, 1775, Concord, Massachusetts."

Liberty cleared his throat and said, "You haven't paid for the trip yet."

"Excuse me?" I asked.

Liberty sighed. "I said, you haven't paid for your trip yet. The price for a round-trip ticket to 1775 is two large carrots. Or one large carrot and a juicy apple. Or a cup of oats. Or—"

"Okay, okay, I get it," I cut in. I reached into Liberty's leather saddlebag and pulled out one large carrot and one fat apple. "Will this be enough?"

"Yes!" Liberty smiled and said, "And on behalf of all of us at Liberty's Getaway Time-Travel Adventures, we hope you enjoy your trip!"

I rolled my eyes and fed Liberty his "payment."

Freedom, Cam, and Tommy were all smiles as they watched from the side of the room.

"Here we go," said Liberty as he swallowed his last bite. "*Rush, rush, rushing to history!*"

From out of nowhere, the time portal swirled in front of us as the sparkling door grew large enough for Liberty to jump through. He rushed forward and we leapt into the middle of the portal.

Suddenly we found ourselves on a hill near a large wild apple tree, overlooking a small valley. It was early springtime but the trees had not fully unpacked their leaves, perhaps fearful of the coming events. It was cold but birds were chirping. A smooth river ran deep and wide through the center of the valley far below. I was sure it was the Concord River. A wooden bridge—the famous Old North Bridge—spanned the watery depths. Homesteads could be seen on either side of the river but the main town of Concord was clearly to the east, below and behind us. Smoke could be seen coming from the town but I couldn't tell what was on fire.

However, the most alarming sight was the Redcoats. Their bright red jackets, white pants, and black boots made the hairs on my arms stand up. The sound of those boots marching across the wooden planks of the bridge matched the rhythm of my own anxious heartbeat. The Redcoats marched until they reached the opposite side from where we stood. Suddenly a British officer shouted the command to stop. The order echoed off the hillside and it sounded like the officer was standing right next to me. About ninety Redcoats halted in unison. Some were still on the bridge but most were nervously scanning the hillsides.

A loud crunching noise came from Liberty's mouth. I wouldn't be surprised if the whole valley had heard it.

"Liberty, shhhhhhhh. This is serious," I whispered firmly.

"What, what? I'm just eating an apple. Very quietly, I might add. This is getting intense. It's like watching a 3-D movie, I always munch on something when I'm at the movies. I mean, I'd rather have popcorn but these apples will have to do. I wonder what those guys on the west hill over there are going to do?"

"What other guys?" I asked, right before I noticed a group of men at the western hilltop facing the Redcoats. They looked eastward toward the bridge. There were only about forty, no, wait, sixty, or should I say one hundred. These had to be Patriots. I quickly snapped a picture of the growing army of Patriot soldiers who were coming up and over the hill and moving toward the Redcoats.

"Seriously, these are really great seats," said Liberty, still munching. "Standing behind this tall hedge and under this apple tree is the perfect hideout. And it's like we're on the fifty-yard line at a football game."

I rolled my eyes and resumed counting the growing militia. There had to be at least four hundred men. I assumed they had heard the bells and had come from all over Massachusetts. And they were still coming. They looked like the farmers in Lexington wearing mismatched clothing. Many wore brown clothing that blended into the hills. But the number of men wasn't the biggest surprise. They actually looked strategic in the way they worked together. Small groups walked slowly and methodically toward the Old North Bridge. Muskets and pistols ready. Fearless and determined.

Upon seeing the Americans approach, the Redcoats realized they were in a horrible position to fight. They quickly tried to scramble back to the eastern side of the bridge. At the same time the Americans looked like they were starting a formation, spreading out on higher ground. Certainly the Americans had the upper hand. The Redcoats stood on and behind the wooden bridge that curved up and over the dark and ominous river.

Liberty grabbed another apple from the tree and asked, "What are they doing?"

"They are coming to fight the British soldiers on the bridge," I said. "They are angry about what happened in Lexington and are coming to protect Concord. They are here to fight for freedom."

"I hope you're getting pictures for Cam and his team," Liberty said. "I think there's something here he could learn from. Might be useful for his next dodgeball game."

Of course, Liberty was right! I quickly took out my phone and started taking pictures.

"Look at the Redcoats, they are squished onto the bridge," Liberty said. "That's not going to be very effective. How are they going to fight like that?"

One Patriot screamed, "Avenge Lexington, my boys! Avenge old Lexington!" His words echoed through the valley, and suddenly the hundreds of Patriots began charging toward the bridge.

Even though Liberty and I were well hidden I instinctively ducked down just to be sure.

Crunch, crunch, crunch, crunched Liberty, trying to be quiet, but failing.

I ignored Liberty and picked out the best pictures I took with my camera. Even though Cam wouldn't see this until we got back to modern day I sent him a text with a note:

Patriots are on Punkatasset Hill, about 300 yards from Redcoats on Old North Bridge. Note: Americans spread out, British close together on and behind bridge.

"This is getting scary," Liberty said nervously. "I think the British are going to start shooting!"

The Patriots steadfastly moved forward. I heard one Patriot yell, "I'm not afraid to go, and I haven't a man who's afraid to go!" His words echoed through the morning air.

Suddenly a shot rang out from the bridge. Instantly, two Patriots fell.

"Fire, for God's sake, fellow soldiers, *fire!*" shouted an American raising his weapon toward the British on the bridge.

They were now about fifty yards apart. Shots rang out from both sides. The Concord River churned and rolled under the bridge, darkly reflecting the turmoil above. Smoke from the muskets was everywhere.

The Patriots continued to push toward the Old North Bridge.

"I think the Patriots are winning," Liberty said excitedly.

Sure enough, the British started to retreat, and the Americans began to cheer as they crossed the bridge. Against all odds, the American underdogs were in fact winning the Battle of Concord.

"Liberty, I think we have the truth about what exactly happened here," I whispered. "Let's jump back to the future."

With a deep breath and a small chomp he said, "*Rush, rush, rushing from history.*"

As the time portal opened again, I felt like I was the white rabbit from *Alice in Wonderland* racing toward the rabbit hole because we were late, late, late for a very important date! We jumped through and the sensation of falling was abruptly interrupted as we landed inside my classroom at Manchester Middle School.

Freedom, Cam, and Tommy were still standing at the side of the room.

"At least you didn't come back with any bullet holes," Tommy said, smiling.

"Ha, ha," I said, dismounting from the saddle. "Pull up some desks and have a seat. We have lots to talk about."

For the next forty-five minutes we discussed all the events that Liberty and I witnessed at the Battle of Concord. Liberty wrote down critical facts on the chalkboard.

Do you remember if the Patriots won at the Battle of Concord? Yes, they did! They crossed the Old North Bridge to defeat the King's soldiers and showed they were willing to keep fighting for freedom.

Concord—Patriots—did not retreat—not scared, courage—spread
out—British stuck on Old North Bridge—British retreat—American
victory—Underdogs.

"Got it. I know how we are going to take on Billy's team next
round," Cam said.

"Find seven hundred kids to take them on?" Tommy asked
sarcastically.

"No, not that. I think we need a change of scenery," Cam said.

"What do you mean?" Freedom asked.

"Remember when we were in Lexington, the British were
really organized and looked like a team. Just like Billy's team.
The Redcoats all wore the same uniforms. They had a system of
fighting that worked best in a large space like Lexington Green.
The Patriots weren't ready for that, so when the Redcoats fired,
they had no chance," Cam said.

"So we are like the Patriots," Tommy asked, "and Billy's team is
like the British?"

I looked on quietly, impressed with their learning and strat-
egizing.

"Yup, exactly," Cam said and walked up to the blackboard.
"Look at this. Here is Billy's team, and here we are. Last game,
we got destroyed 'cause Billy had a stronger team that was more
organized. They spread out and tagged us all at once." He drew
a circle on the board. "Now look. If we put them all in a small
space we have a chance, plus we might be able to get a few more
people, but we don't have much time."

"It's still going to be tough," Tommy said.

"You're right, Tommy, it's all about planning ahead," Cam

said. "That's where you come in, Tommy. You will be my Paul Revere—ready to spread the alarm and gather as many people as you can to fight with us."

"Got it," Tommy said, flexing an arm.

"Freedom, I need your skills, too," Cam said. "You will be my Dr. Warren, the superplanner—and we need an awesome plan."

"Got it!" Freedom said, standing up. She started scratching down some notes furiously.

"All I know is that we aren't going to make the same mistake twice," Cam said. "We may be the underdogs but this time we are going to beat that bully."

"I like the way you're thinking," said Tommy.

"Yeah, I do, too," said Freedom.

"Me, too," said Liberty. "I do like dodgeball Cam-I-Am, but I will not eat green eggs and ham! Seriously, blech! First of all, what's up with the green food coloring? And second, eggs come from a chicken and ham comes from a pig and they're both farm animals, which means we're practically cousins. I am *not* eating my cousins! Sheesh."

I tried to ignore Liberty's commentary and said, "Sounds like you guys have the start of a good plan, but you are missing one vital component."

"What's that?" Tommy asked.

"You need an upper hand, something that turns the battle for the underdog, some special secret sauce," I said.

"I think I may have the secret sauce," Freedom said, looking at her notepad full of lines and scribbles.

"What is it?" Tommy asked.

Freedom cupped her hand over her mouth and whispered

it to Tommy. His eyes went wide with doubt and a little bit of worry.

"I don't think that will work," Tommy said reluctantly.

"What is it?" Cam asked.

Tommy whispered in Cam's ear.

Cam looked doubtful as well. "I don't know, seems like a long shot."

"True," Freedom said. "But if it did work don't you think it could be a game changer?"

"Probably," Cam said. "Unless it backfires."

"Yeah, it could totally backfire," Tommy said.

"I still think it's worth a try," Freedom said.

"Is someone going to tell me what your secret strategy is?" I asked curiously.

"It's probably better if you don't know," Freedom said.

Both boys nodded in agreement.

"Does this strategy of yours involve Liberty?" I asked suspiciously. "Because if it does I really better know."

"Oh! Oh! Am I part of a top-secret mission?" Liberty asked, jumping up and down like he had to go to the bathroom.

"Actually, no, you're not," Freedom said.

Both boys shook their heads, confirming Freedom's reply. Liberty frowned.

I eyed them all suspiciously. "Very well," I said, smiling. "I trust you know what you're doing." And I really hoped they did.

Chapter 7

I had *butterflies in* my stomach as I entered the military base gym. The second-round dodgeball game would start in a few minutes. Earlier that day, Cam had sent a message to Billy and insisted that the game be changed to the indoor court.

Even better! texted Billy. I can't wait to see you bounce off the hardwood floors.

Indeed, the floors felt especially hard as I walked along the sidelines to join Cam, Tommy, and Freedom. Four other student recruits that I didn't know stood with them.

"Hey, I made us some uniforms," Freedom said, handing out blue T-shirts to the team. On the front of the shirt were the letters E, A, G, L, E, S.

"Thank you Freedom, these look awesome! Eagles is a cool name," Cam said.

"I didn't have a lot of time so they're not the best but at

least we have something that says we're a team. Mr. Revere paid for the T-shirts and supplies," said Freedom.

"Wow! Thanks, Mr. Revere!" cheered Cam and Tommy and the other kids.

"It was the least I could do," I said, blushing. "I figured if John Hancock could invest in the early American war effort, then I could invest in you." I winked.

"Mahahaha! Those are the dorkiest shirts ever," Billy said, pacing across his side of the court. "Ha! We'll use them to mop the floor after we win! You'll be wearing new LOSER shirts by then anyway!"

"I think you'd better worry about your own team, Billy," Cam said, walking straight up to the centerline and looking up at him.

Billy glared down at Cam and pushed him backward. "You have a big mouth for being such a small fry!"

Cam was unbelievably brave. The protective teacher in me wanted to run over and break it up before the game even started, but I restrained myself.

Suddenly, I realized that Ed was missing. I searched the bleachers on either side of the court. There were even more spectators than last time waiting for the game to start but no sign of Ed. Where could he be?

"Hey, Eagles, come over here, gather around," Cam said, waving his team to the sideline. "Huddle in; you, too, Mr. Revere." As we all formed a tight circle Cam said, "I want to thank all of you for coming. I know some of you might be nervous, but we can't let Billy see that. I mean we may look like underdogs, but we're really the unstoppable Eagles!" he said.

Cam was maturing before my eyes. He took to the leadership role like Liberty to a carrot.

"We got this," he said confidently. "Let's go win!"

The other kids looked at Cam with wide eyes, hanging on every word he said. They all put their hands in the middle, lifted them, and yelled, "Go Eagles!!"

I stood close to the sidelines. There were a lot of kids in the bleachers, cheering. Some were pointing at my outfit, probably thinking I was the official mascot. I wished I was wearing a T-shirt that said FEAR THE REVERE!

Freedom asked, "Have you seen Ed? I'm getting nervous. We need everyone, to make our plan work."

"He's in the bathroom," Tommy said. "He's getting dressed."

"What could possibly take him so long?" Freedom complained, wringing her hands. "He just has to put on the T-shirt I made for him!"

A bright green flash caught the corner of my eye. I looked over across the gym court to see Ed on the opposite side. What's he wearing? I thought to myself. I didn't want to laugh but he looked absolutely hysterical. Thank goodness Liberty was at the horse spa or he would be on the floor right now rolling on his back with laughter.

Ed came bounding over to our sideline, very much like Little Liberty! He was wearing shiny green kneepads and large elbow pads. He wore a bicycle helmet strapped to his head and welding glasses over his eyes. His sneakers squeaked with every step.

"Ha! Who's the green blob?" Billy doubled over laughing. "Oh, I get it. You tried to recruit a Teenage Mutant Ninja Turtle. But all you got was a teenage mutant Brussels sprout." His team buckled over laughing and pointing at Ed.

Cam very admirably didn't skip a beat and waved Ed into the huddle.

"Don't touch me. These green sweats are armed and ready," Ed called out.

"If you say so," said Tommy, confused.

"Nice helmet," said Cam, winking. "Seriously, I'm really glad you made it, Ed. It's going to take all we've got to defeat these bullies. Does everyone know what to do?"

"I do," said Ed with enough enthusiasm for the entire team. "I studied all night!"

Tommy rolled his eyes and was about to pat Ed on the shoulder, but Ed slipped away just in time. "I told you, no touchy! Unless you want to stick with me for the rest of the game."

Cam started giving out instructions. "Okay, Freedom, I need you to take the back left position. You four spread out. Ed take the center, and Tommy, I need you to roam behind Ed like a quarterback, and don't get hit! As soon as the whistle blows we'll take our positions. Hey, Freedom, what about the secret plan? Is that still going to happen?"

Freedom turned from Cam to Tommy and asked, "Did you do your part?"

Tommy sighed and nodded. "Yes, but I hope I don't regret it."

Cam looked at his watch. "We're almost out of time. Without Freedom's plan our chances of—"

Cam was interrupted by the sound of music coming from somewhere outside the gym. It got louder as the gym doors opened and the lyrics blasted, *This girl is on fire*. A girl wearing a red cheerleading outfit walked in like she owned the place. She flipped her blond ponytail from side to side as she made her way into the room. Her bright red fingernails matched her outfit perfectly. As she walked across the floor, my jaw dropped when

I realized who it was. Elizabeth! She was followed by her perfectly peppy cheerleading squad.

In a matter of seconds, Elizabeth walked over to Cam and his
friends. She looked at Tommy and said, "Hi, Thomas, I hope you
know how much I enjoyed receiving your phone call. You know
there aren't many things that would get me away from my summer beach house and onto this, this . . ." She scrunched her nose.
"What do you call it?"

"It's a military base," Cam clarified.

"Whatever," Elizabeth said, completely disinterested.

Elizabeth flipped her hair the other way and said, "By the way,
those guards at the front gate need a total fashion makeover.
Anyway, like I said, we're here to cheer." She stepped closer to
Tommy and whispered, "Don't forget our agreement. I do you a
favor, like cheering for your team, and you do me a favor."

Tommy squirmed a little and replied, "But you haven't told me
what the favor is."

"You'll know soon enough," Elizabeth teased. "By the way . . ."
She paused like she just realized where she was. "Where's your
football team?"

"We're not playing football. We're playing dodgeball," Tommy
said. "And this is my team." He pointed to the seven players
around him, including Ed.

Elizabeth scanned the motley crew but shielded her eyes
when she saw Ed's outfit. "And I thought Freedom dressed badly."

Freedom rolled her eyes in disapproval.

"Seriously, your raggle-taggle clothes are so last year, except
for you, Mr. Revere. You're clothes are so . . . so . . ."

"Classical?" I offered.

"No, that's *not* it," she replied. "They look so . . . prehistoric."

I could only laugh at her attempt at an insult.

"Elizabeth," Cam interrupted, "I have no idea what *raggle-taggle* means but we need you to cheer. And that means cheering for Freedom, too."

Elizabeth turned to her squad and said, "Girls, this is going to be harder than I thought."

Suddenly Billy was towering behind Elizabeth with his hands on his hips. Taunting, he asked, "What's with all the primped poodles? Camera and his little birdie players can't join you for a tea party because *I'm* having them for lunch, so beat it!"

Elizabeth slowly turned to face Billy. It looked like laser beams might shoot from her eyes. The other cheerleaders stared menacingly at Billy as they stepped up behind their captain. Elizabeth looked up into his face and carefully said, "I don't know who you are, but you'd better get your loser self over to the other side of the court or this pack of *poodles* is going to eat you up and spit you out." She hissed, shoving her red claws just inches from his face. The sudden move startled Billy and he stumbled backward.

"Whatever," he said as he waved her off and walked back to his team.

With puppy dog eyes, Ed bravely stepped up to Elizabeth and said, "My name is Ed. You must be Athena—goddess of wisdom and war. And your beauty shines like a supernova."

Before Elizabeth could reply, Cam gently pulled Ed behind him and smiled at Elizabeth. Cam said, "Thanks for coming, you are a big help."

"I know," she replied. She looked over at Billy's team. "I sure hope you have a game plan because this could get ugly, real fast."

The referee blew his whistle and the kids ran to their places on the court.

"Don't forget, stay focused. No fear. Remember the plan!" Cam said.

I was nervous for Cam and his team. Would their plan beat Billy's teamwork?

I gave Cam a thumbs-up right before the whistle blew again.

The narrow court didn't give Billy's team much room to maneuver. He had too many players racing forward. They bumped into each other as they scrambled to get a ball. Cam's team with fewer players was faster and snatched their balls first. A player from Billy's team fired his ball across the centerline. It hit one of Cam's friends on the shin before he could turn around to throw his own ball. Billy's team was all smiles.

"Fire!" Cam shouted. In unison, seven balls hurtled toward Billy's team. The smaller court made it difficult for Billy's crowded team to dodge the incoming balls. It was just like the Old North Bridge at the battle of Concord! Too many soldiers and not enough room to do anything. Several of Billy's players were hit and knocked out of the game. Cam's strategy was working.

Back and forth balls flew across the centerline. Billy had lost half his players and was no longer smiling. In fact, he wiped his brow as he counted who was left on his team.

On the Eagles, only Cam, Tommy, Freedom, Ed, and one younger boy remained.

Billy shouted to his team, "Fire on the green blob!"

Three members of Billy's team threw their balls at the same time. They were targeting Ed! He was a sitting duck. No way could he avoid the rapid fire and stop all of those balls from beaming him!

To my surprise, the balls didn't hit him and bounce off. They stuck to him like glue! Two balls stuck to one side and one to the other. "Genius!" I shouted, suddenly self-conscious about how loud my voice was. I realized this was all part of the plan! The silly green suit wasn't so silly after all!

Ed spun around once, then twice, and finally released the rubber ball as it streaked forward with a wicked spin. It curved into an unsuspecting player and bounced off to hit a second and then a third before finally hitting the floor. Elizabeth's cheerleaders shouted wildly, overpowering the crowd. You could tell by the faces on Billy's team that they were starting to panic.

"C'mon, guys!" Cam yelled. "We can do this, let's go!"

Balls continued to fly back and forth in a haze. Finally it came down to two against two. Billy and another big kid on one side, Cam and big green Ed on the other.

"C'mon, Cam, c'mon, Ed!" Freedom yelled from the sidelines.

Billy sent a ball blazing across the centerline toward Ed, who already had about three or four balls stuck to his green suit. The ball was too low to stick to Ed and ricocheted off his right shoe toward the sideline.

"Ahhhhh," Elizabeth shouted in a high-pitched yell. "You did not just do that," she sneered, glaring across the court at Billy.

I leaned toward Freedom and said, "Wow, I think Elizabeth is genuinely upset that Billy hit Ed with the ball."

Freedom looked at me like I was from some other planet. "She's not mad about that. She's ticked off because the ball that Billy threw just broke one of her nails."

Elizabeth threw down her pom-poms and stepped onto the court as Ed waddled off to the sideline.

"You can't add players!" Billy shouted.

Cam brightened. "I didn't. She's our backup, just like in the Battle of Concord."

Billy gave a confused look. Flustered, he said, "But I don't have any backup."

Cam gave the biggest grin I'd ever seen and said, "Too bad, you should have *planned* for that!" He gave me a quick glance and a quicker thumbs-up.

Dr. Warren would be proud, I thought.

Elizabeth snapped her fingers and her entire squad of cheerleaders walked onto the court and picked up the remaining rubber balls. This definitely got Billy's attention.

Cam noted, "Looks like your best choice is to retreat."

Beads of sweat rolled from Billy's forehead. He stared at the team of fresh Eagles.

Tommy pulled on my jacket and whispered, "Mr. Revere, this is just like the Battle of Concord, right? Just like Cam said. Didn't the Americans get fresh soldiers and didn't the Redcoats retreat out of the city?"

I nodded. "That's right. And if Billy's smart he'll accept Cam's offer."

Billy sneered and called to Cam, "This isn't over. Your team is still lame." He turned to his dejected players and said, "Let's get out of here." All the red shirts followed him outside.

As he walked away, Elizabeth chucked her ball at Billy and it hit him in the back of the head. He whipped around ready to pound someone into the ground. When he saw it was Elizabeth she shouted, "That's for breaking my nail!"

"Have fun wearing the LOSER shirts!" Tommy shouted with a wide grin.

Billy grunted and stormed out of the building. Cheers erupted throughout the bleachers. I raced into center court as if my team had just won the Super Bowl. I was immensely proud of their courage and planning and creativity and unity. Cam's leadership almost brought a tear to my eye.

Instead, I gave all of the Eagles a high five and said, "Congratulations, guys, you looked amazing out there. You should be very proud of yourselves!"

"Did you see how Ed got all the balls stuck to him and then spun and knocked out three players in a single shot?" Freedom asked.

"Absolutely. That was the best part, and the cheering from Elizabeth and her cheer squad got our team fired up," Cam said.

"Yeah, but Cam is the real hero," said Tommy. "He believed in us from the very start!"

"I couldn't have done it without everyone doing their part," said Cam. "And now look at us. We started out as the underdogs, but now we're the top dogs!" He gave a huge smile as he high-fived Tommy.

"Where's Elizabeth?" asked Cam.

"She took off as soon as the game ended," said Freedom. "I overheard her say that the gym was starting to smell like a pair of smelly socks."

"Hey, great idea!" said Tommy. "I'll start wearing stinky socks to school. Maybe that will send her a message."

"I'm afraid that will send everyone a message," I joked.

The team gathered their bags and headed for the door. As we

all exited the gym I started to think about our next adventure. I couldn't help it. History was calling to me. I blurted out, "Freedom, I want you to know that I was really impressed with your innovative secret plan. Inviting Elizabeth and her cheerleaders and saving them as backup players was genius. Dr. Warren would be proud."

"Thanks, Mr. Revere," said Freedom, blushing.

"And, Tommy, I was very impressed by your bravery and willingness to sacrifice one for the team. You remind me of Paul Revere. Oh, and good luck with whatever favor you're doing for Elizabeth," I said with a smirk.

"You guys all owe me," said Tommy.

"And, Cam, I was especially impressed with your leadership during the game. In fact, you remind me of George Washington."

"Huh?" Cam looked back at me a bit confused. "I do?"

"You absolutely do! So much so that I think we should visit him. I have a feeling you would really like getting to know George Washington better."

"Sure, I'm up for it! I want to find out what the first President of the United States has in common with me!" Cam laughed.

"You both probably snore," Freedom teased.

"Oops, I almost forgot," said Tommy abruptly. "I told Ed I'd help him out of his green alien outfit. I bet he's still in the locker room waiting for me. Gotta run. See you guys later." He jogged back to the gym.

"Do you need any help?" I called after Tommy.

"No, that's okay, my dad is coming to pick me up. In fact, I see his car pulling up now. I'll make sure Ed gets home. See ya," Tommy said with a wave.

Cam's face went from smiling ear to ear to a bit of a frown. For a second, I wondered why. Then I realized that Tommy had just mentioned his dad.

"You know, Cam, your dad will be very happy to hear how well you did today. He'll be very proud of you, just like I am." I patted Cam on the back. He didn't say anything but I could tell he wished his dad had been there to see his win. "I know your mom is mighty proud. If she didn't have to take your sister to the dentist, you know she would have been here. She asked me to take lots of video!"

"Thank you, yeah, I know," Cam said. His tone was softer than before. I walked with Cam back to the cafeteria and let him know I would see him tomorrow morning at nine at Manchester Middle School.

"Congratulations again, you did awesome!" I said, giving one last high five.

The next morning, Liberty spent most of the ride to the school telling me about his day at the horse spa. I was half-listening, half-thinking about what I would say to George Washington.

"And then this woman named Helga came in and gave me a massage," said Liberty. "Wow! She really knows her pressure points. Anyway, she only works part-time at the spa, and the rest of the time she's training to compete in a hammer-throwing competition. I'm just saying I am totally stress-free and ready to time-jump. Seriously, I'm so loosey-goosey I could jump to the Jurassic period!"

We soon arrived at Manchester Middle School, where Cam and Freedom were waiting for us on the grass near the track, our usual meeting spot.

"Good morning, Mr. Revere and Liberty!" Freedom said excitedly.

"Good morning. Where's Tommy?" I asked. "Let me guess, he slept in."

"Nope," said Cam. "He has to spend the day with Eliza-brat!"

"Yeah," said Freedom. "He's super-bummed. Elizabeth is redeeming her favor today."

"What flavor?" asked Liberty curiously. "My favorite flavor is asparagus. But I also like pumpkin and cloves. Hmm, I want to redeem a flavor, too!"

"Not a *flavor*," Freedom corrected. "A *favor*."

"Yeah," Cam said, "he owes Elizabeth a favor. And she asked him to make a picture album for her and fill it with pictures of himself."

"That's a little creepy," said Liberty.

Freedom added, "I think she just likes to torture him because she knows an album is the last thing Tommy would like to do . . . ever."

"Well, I'm glad he's sticking to his agreement. Good for him," I said.

"So, are we really going to visit George Washington?" asked Cam with a big grin.

"Absolutely," I said. "But first, I want to test your memories. Remember where we left off the last time the two of you went back in time?"

Freedom thought for a minute and answered, "We met Dr. Warren! And Cam almost got cut in the arm. And a boy came in and told some spy news so Dr. Warren set in motion his big plan for Team America like sending Paul Revere to tell everyone in the countryside to get ready."

"Exactly right, spot on," I said. "And what was Paul Revere telling everyone in the countryside to get ready for?"

"Get ready for breakfast or lunch or dinner!" said Liberty. "I love when I hear those words."

I grabbed an apple from Liberty's saddlebag as Cam answered, "When the British soldiers started to move, Paul Revere rode to warn everyone to get ready for a British invasion."

"All right, smarty-pants," said Liberty as he chewed his apple, "bonus question! Why were there two lanterns hanging in the Old North Church?"

"So the people on the other side of the river could get ready to defend themselves," stated Freedom confidently.

"Yeah, one lit lantern if the British were leaving Boston through Boston Neck. And two lit lanterns if they were leaving Boston by sea, over the Charles River," beamed Cam. "We got this, Liberty. You can't stump us. We were there!"

How many kids can say that? I wondered.

"Exactly right!" I said, pulling out a map of Boston and surrounding areas of Massachusetts. I pointed to the map and asked, "Who can find Charlestown?"

"I can! Right there," Freedom said, pointing.

"Correct. We went from Dr. Warren's house in Boston, here. Then across the Charles River to Charlestown, here. Then Cam and Tommy rode Little Liberty up here toward Lexington," I said, pointing to spots on the map. "This is where we saw the Battle of Lexington."

"I remember that battle," said Cam somberly. "The Americans lost in that big field!"

"Just like we lost our first dodgeball game," said Freedom.

I added, "But America won the very next battle, in Concord."

"Oh yeah, you and Liberty time-jumped to the Battle of Concord, right? That's where we won and forced the British to retreat all the way to Boston!" said Cam.

"Just like Billy's team during the dodgeball game," Freedom said.

"Exactly right," I said. "And today, we are going to Philadelphia. You can't see it on this map but it is southwest of Boston. We're going to meet up with George Washington right after he was appointed at the Second Continental Congress as commander in chief of the new Patriot army."

"Does it have a drive-through?" Liberty asked.

"The Congress? Um, no," I said with an eyebrow raised, not even sure what Liberty was talking about. "But I do want you to drive through time and find General Washington in Philadelphia. You might want to check around the stables near the State House. He loved to be near his horses."

"I knew there was a reason I liked that man," said Liberty.

I grabbed the colonial clothes out of Liberty's saddle and the kids slipped them over their modern-day clothes. Soon they looked the part and no one would ever know they were from the twenty-first century. When Freedom and Cam were on Liberty's back I said, "We're headed to Philadelphia, June 14th, 1775."

Eagerly, Liberty called out, *"Rush, rush, rushing to history."*

The swirling time door opened out of thin air. We raced forward and jumped through the center. Instantly, we were clearly in a different time and place.

The stables were filled with hay and smelled of wood and horses. Saddles lined the walls and leather bridles hung from pegs on the wall.

Liberty's uncanny ability to track down exceptional Americans did not disappoint. As we turned a corner to one of the stables we saw a man feeding a handful of hay to a beautiful white horse.

"Is that George Washington?" Cam asked. The man was tall, with broad shoulders and looked to be in his forties. He wore a crisp linen shirt with a cream vest and a navy blue jacket with golden tassels on each shoulder. He wore tall black leather boots that reached just below his knee and a sheathed sword hung from the side of his hip.

"I think so, Cam, this is really exciting," I whispered.

George Washington smiled and greeted us. "I feel like we've met before," he said.

"Yes, we have," I replied. "At the First Continental Congress. We ate meat pies with your fellow Patriots Patrick Henry, John Adams, and Samuel Adams."

"Ah, yes," said Washington. "Rush Revere, is it? I could never forget your beautiful horse." Washington pulled out another handful of hay from a nearby bucket and fed it to Liberty.

"That's right," I said, smiling, delighted to know he remembered us. "And these are two more of my students, Cameron and Freedom."

"A pleasure," George Washington said. At first he seemed to be a man of few words, yet as Cam showed an interest he started to say more. "Come and sit with me," said Washington as he led us to a nearby bench. He sat down and pulled a map from his coat pocket."

When Cam and Freedom were sitting beside him on either side, he asked, "Do you like maps?"

Cam and Freedom nodded enthusiastically.

"So do I," said Washington. He unfolded the map until it covered his lap. The creased parchment was a map of New England.

This man was the commander in chief of the Continental Army. Can you name him? It is George Washington, a true patriot who led the First Continental Army during the American Revolutionary War. After the war, he became the first president of the United States of America.

There were notes and names and markings all around the edges written in ink. Washington looked at both kids and said, "I often think late at night about this war. In the morning I write those thoughts down."

"Like what kinds of things do you think about?" Cam asked.

Washington smiled. "All sorts of things, Cameron. I think about how to best prepare our army. I know that we do not have as many soldiers as the King does. I know that our soldiers are not as prepared or as organized. I know we don't have the same funding and we lack the weapons and gunpowder. But I believe there are solutions for those problems. I just have to think long and hard about what they are."

Eagerly, Cam said, "I know what you mean about thinking long and hard. I was preparing for this dodgeball game and . . ."

Washington interrupted, "Dodgeball? I have not heard of this."

Cam replied, "Oh, it's this new game that kids are playing now."

"Yeah," Freedom said. "It's really, really, new."

Cam smiled and said, "I planned and thought about how to beat this really strong team and it kept me up for a lot of nights. I couldn't sleep at all! But we finally figured it out."

George Washington nodded slowly and intently asked, "And did you beat this strong opponent?"

"Yeah, we did. The planning worked," replied Cam as Freedom nodded vigorously. Cam added, "It really pays to think things through. I'm sure you'll receive the answers you need to your toughest problems."

Washington softly laughed and said, "Thank you, Cameron. Your faith gives me confidence."

This is another portrait of George Washington,
this time in formal non-military clothing.

"It's a real honor to meet you, Mr. President," Cam said, suddenly realizing that George Washington doesn't become President of the United States until years later. Freedom quickly looked at me to see if I noticed Cam's blunder.

Perplexed, Washington asked, "Did you say 'Mr. President'? Well, I suppose I am the president of the Army. But the official title that Congress has given me is Commander in Chief of the Continental Army."

Of course, at this time in history George Washington didn't know he would one day be the President of the United States of America. He was a man of great humility, and now he was in charge of the entire Continental Army, more than thirteen thousand men, the new American army.

"I really like the title Commander in Chief, it still sounds really important," Freedom offered.

"Thank you, Freedom," Washington said. "But a name and title like President or Commander or General is not nearly as important as doing what needs to be done to accomplish this country's greatest mission. I want to do the best I can to fight for freedom. These young Patriot soldiers have sacrificed so much in the fight so far. I look to God to give me the strength to lead well and honorably."

"So how do you think you can win?" asked Cam. "How will you defeat a bigger, more powerful opponent?" Cam was like an investigative journalist who was really digging in and asking the juicy questions.

"It will be a long and hard struggle," Washington replied. "The odds are most certainly against us and we are truly overpowered. I must somehow make our soldiers believe that no matter what obstacles are in our way, we can win with determination and the passion to do so. The moment we give up is the moment we lose. I must find a way for my men to find their deepest strength and remember what they are fighting for—freedom! God willing, we will endure and triumph," Washington said. "I just hope to be a small part of this glorious cause."

Cam was focused on Washington's every word. He was absorbing everything and kept asking questions.

"Where did you find the men to join the army?" Cam asked. "The King's troops are so scary, it is amazing that so many are joining."

George Washington replied, "You are such a bright young man. That is a wonderful question and one of the things I am most focused on. They are all fighting for their freedom and their families' freedom. They come from all different backgrounds, some descended from the first colonists, many from New England, and new immigrants from Europe. Some are former slaves of African descent. We have sailors, farmers, and teachers. All are volunteers. They come from small towns and cities and many are from the same family. It is an incredible group of men."

All of a sudden I noticed that Liberty was missing. What was he up to now? I wondered. Knowing Liberty, it could be anything under the sun.

Timidly, Freedom spoke up and asked Washington, "Are you scared?"

Washington looked directly at Freedom and said, "All I fear is that I won't do enough to serve my country."

"What about this winter?" asked Freedom, shivering as she thought about it. "I hate cold weather. I can't imagine having to live and fight in it all the time."

"Yes, come winter, we will be freezing," said Washington. "But the men have a fire in their stomachs, and that will carry them through."

"So, what's the next step, sir?" asked Cam with bright and curious eyes.

"I have already begun gathering more men and preparing them for war. We will head to a gathering place near Boston. Near a place called Cambridge." He pointed to a place on the map still in his lap. "Right here. I expect to rally thirteen thousand, six hundred American soldiers. We will show those Redcoats that we will not back down."

"I can't wait!" Cam said.

Finally, Liberty walked out of the stables with a mischievous look on his face. His cheeks were puffed out like he just ate hundreds of gumballs. He must have found the stable kitchen or a bucket of hay!

"There's something special about your horse," General Washington said with a smile.

"Why, thank you, he is certainly one of a kind!" I said.

"Speaking of horses," said Washington, "I must be on my way from here soon. Before I go, may I request a favor?"

"Anything, sir," Cam said before I had a chance to answer.

I wondered and worried a little what Cam had just committed us to do.

George Washington stood up and folded a piece of parchment paper to look like a letter going into an envelope. "I wrote down some thoughts that I hope will inspire the young men to keep fighting on. I know their days are long and it must become very hard for them to keep going. These words are only words but I hope they help in some small way."

"Could you take this letter to the men at Bunker Hill? Give it to the first general or captain you find."

I paused for a minute, not knowing what to say to George Washington. Would I be changing the events of history if I agreed? I couldn't say no to a man I admired so much. If I did, what kind of Patriot would he think I was? He must have inspired many people in one way or another so really it wouldn't be changing history.

Liberty saw the look on my face and started to snort. The sound brought me out of my temporary haze and I responded to Washington, "I would be honored, sir."

"You are fine Patriots of the highest order. Thank you, Revere," General Washington said, firmly shaking my hand. "Now I must be on my way. Time is a cherished possession."

As George Washington walked to his horse he noticed Freedom braiding a piece of the light mane. It was an intricate braid made with the skill of a master weaver.

"I'm impressed. It is beautiful," said Washington.

"Thanks," said Freedom, blushing.

"Whenever I look at this braid I will remember it was a gift from Freedom—your name is a word that will forever give me hope." He lifted himself onto his saddle and said, "Godspeed, Rush Revere. And, Cameron, keep doing what you're doing. America needs leaders like you. I look forward to our next visit." He spurred his horse and waved. We all waved back and Cam, especially, watched George Washington ride all the way down the road until he disappeared.

Freedom ran over to me and asked with a worried look, "What is Bunker Hill? Are we going to a battle?"

"Well, yes, the Battle of Bunker Hill is one of the most

important battles of the American Revolution. In fact, it is really the first major battle of the revolution. I really didn't plan on us going until General Washington asked us to do a favor for him. Would you rather we go home to modern day first?"

"No way, I'm not going home. This is way too important," Cam strongly said.

"I don't really want to be in a battle. It's really scary, you guys," said Freedom.

Liberty chimed in: "I'm thinking in exchange for going, I should get two extra flavors, uh, I mean favors. First, another massage from Helga, and second, two all-you-can-eat buffets."

"That's actually three favors," I pointed out.

"It's not that I don't want to go," said Freedom, looking disappointed. "It's just that I'm a little scared after all the stories I heard from Tommy about the Battle of Lexington."

"Don't worry, Freedom, I will protect you," said Liberty. "If there is any danger, you can jump on my back and we are outta there!" Liberty said in heroic fashion.

"Thanks, Liberty. That does make me feel a little better."

"Liberty is exactly right," I reassured her. "I, too, will make sure that you stay safe," I promised.

"Cam, did you hear that? I do believe I got an 'exactly right.' Please deposit that in my compliment bank," Liberty said with a wide grin as we all laughed. Even Freedom giggled a little.

"All right," said Freedom. "I'm in. But I really am staying close to Liberty!"

Chapter 8

So, *Mr. Revere*, right now who's winning?" asked Cam. We were standing outside the stables, and the wind was picking up.

"What do you mean?" I asked, curious to know what he was thinking.

"Well, the American team lost the Battle of Lexington Green, right?" Cam asked.

"Not to mention we almost lost Tommy," Liberty mumbled. I gave him *the look*.

Cam continued: "And a few hours after Lexington the American team won at the Battle of Concord, right?"

"Yes, that's correct," I replied. The wind was blowing heavily now and little bits of hay were flying all around.

"So is it one–one?" Freedom asked. I now understood: they were comparing the early Revolutionary War battles to game tallies in sports.

"Yes, you could say that. It's also fair to say that by

winning the Battle of Concord the American team had a little more confidence and motivation to keep fighting for freedom," I replied, thrilled with their analysis.

"Ooh, that's kinda like our team playing Billy the Bully. I mean after the first game we thought we were totally toast but with a new game plan we had more confidence," Cam added.

"Hummm hummmm." Liberty cleared his throat and said, "I'll jump in here. We are heading to the tiebreaker at the Battle of Bunker Hill and I know who wins." Then he whispered, "But I can't say anything because Captain Grouchy-Pants hates when I ruin the endings."

I forced a smile and said, "Thank you, Liberty, for restraining yourself. Now then, let's time-jump so Cam and Freedom can find out who wins . . . for themselves."

My plan was to time-jump three days forward to a hilltop in Charlestown. Since we were still in 1775, I assured Liberty that jumping only a few days ahead instead of a few centuries would be a piece of cake for him.

"Got it, no problemo, you can count on me, mum's the word," said Liberty with a wink.

"Here we go, " I said, hoping Liberty would stay focused. "Let's get going on our adventure!"

As we raced toward the time portal Liberty said, "*Rush, rush, rushing to history.*" Freedom and Cam were riding on Liberty and I was trailing close behind.

I yelled, "Charlestown, Massachusetts, June 17, 1775, Breed's Hill!"

"Breed's Hill?" Freedom asked in a confused tone through the sound of the wind. "I think General Washington told us Bunker Hill."

We landed on a grassy hill overlooking Charlestown. The sun was just starting to come up and there was a morning chill in the air. From the hill we could see across the Charles River to Boston. There was water on every side in front, below us, and land to our backs. Huge British warships were anchored in the water between Charlestown and Boston. From the hill, they looked like small dots, but I knew they were huge navy warships the size of football fields.

"Where's the cake?" Liberty asked as he searched left and right.

"What are you talking about?" I asked, confused.

Liberty clarified: "You said jumping to Charlestown from Philadelphia should be a piece of cake for me. I sure hope it's a carrot cake."

I didn't have the heart to tell him there wasn't any cake.

Freedom kindly replied, "Liberty, it's just an expression. When something's a piece of cake it means it's easy. Just like carrying me on your back is a breeze or a snap or a cakewalk."

Liberty criticized: "Who in their right mind would walk on a cake? Oh, sure, it might be easy but that's just rude, messy, and crazy talk!"

"Mr. Revere, are you sure we are in the right place?" Freedom asked. "Didn't General Washington say Bunker Hill?"

"Well done, time-traveler genius," I said. "That is absolutely right. It is called the Battle of Bunker Hill but it was actually fought on Breed's Hill. An interesting historical nugget!" Cam and Freedom did not look particularly impressed with the nugget. Their expressions seemed to say, That makes no sense at all.

Waving them in toward me, I said, "Huddle over here, guys.

Let me bring you up to speed. Yes, you, too, Liberty. Leaders of the Patriot forces in Boston learned that the British army was planning to take over the hills surrounding the city."

"Get out of here—were they playing finders-keepers?" Liberty chimed in.

"You could call it that. The British knew if they could take over these hills, plus the waterways down below us, and the land, there would be no stopping them! They would take over the city of Boston and all surrounding areas of Massachusetts and the American team would lose. But . . ."

Liberty interrupted. "Hold on one sec. I promise, fear not, I won't give anything away but I have just a little something to add that I picked up playing trivia."

Knowing I didn't really have a choice, I reluctantly agreed. "Go ahead."

"When the Americans heard from their spies that the British wanted to get the hills first," Liberty said proudly, "they said no way, no how! We are going to take over the hill first, finders-keepers style."

"Yes, exactly right!" I said, relieved Liberty was staying on track.

We had a second of silence as we looked around. Through the quiet we began to hear a rhythmic sound, *thud, clack, swoosh, thud, clack, swoosh.*

"What's that noise?" Freedom asked.

Liberty replied with enthusiasm, "Okay, okay, so are we done with finders-keepers? Wait, wait, now we're playing one of those word games where we guess the noise, right? Okay, let me concentrate. I'll guess first. Is it animal, vegetable, or mineral?"

Ignoring Liberty's conversation with himself, Freedom

listened carefully to the noise. "It sounds like metal against rock," she said.

Liberty mused, "Okay, so mineral. Let's see. Is it smaller than a bread box?"

Cam chimed in: "Yeah, I hear it, too. It sounds like digging. Lots of people digging."

"Hmm," pondered Liberty. "You say digging? Maybe mining. In that case, my guess is gold? Or maybe silver?"

I said, "I'm pretty sure the sound you are hearing is men digging a fort known as a *redoubt*."

"What? Did you just make that up?" said Liberty, narrowing his eyes.

Ignoring Liberty, I led the team closer to the fort. We got there as the final wall was being built. The American Patriots must have been working all night to build this fort before the British could find out in the morning.

"Man, I wish Tommy could see this. He's totally into fort building. I mean maybe not the hard-labor part, he kinda bails from hard work, but the fort building part he'd love," Cam said. Around us more than a hundred men were digging, carrying dirt, and doing other jobs. They looked exhausted, dirty, and sweaty, and were trying to catch their breath.

"See all those big ships down there in the water? Well, the British leaders probably just woke up to find the Patriots had quickly built a fort up here on Breed's Hill. They were shocked! My guess is they want to take the hill and are planning their strategy right now," I said.

"Mr. Revere, do you think a cannonball from one of those ships in the harbor could reach this fort way up here?" asked Freedom nervously.

"I bet they could," said Cam.

"Me, too!" Liberty joined in.

Just then a flash of light and the sound of an explosion erupted from the side of one of the warships.

"Oh no! Is that what I think it is?" panicked Freedom.

Sure enough, cannonballs started flying toward the fort from the ships below. The ground shook and there was dust flying everywhere.

"Hurry, duck behind that wall!" I yelled, my heart racing.

"I'm scared!" Freedom cried out. We all fell to the ground with our backs against the earthen wall.

"Everything is going to be okay," I said, very nervous on the inside.

Freedom sat frozen on the ground and clung to one of Liberty's legs. "I'll protect you," Liberty said, keeping the promise he made.

"Mr. Revere, I hear a lot cannon noise but I don't feel many cannonballs hitting the fort," said Cam.

I stood up to see over the wall and said, "Oh no! That's because they're hitting the city of Charlestown."

In what seemed like a few minutes Charlestown was on fire! Huge billows of smoke rose high into the once cloudless sky.

"Wait, Charlestown? That's where you guys met Paul Revere before he started his midnight ride, right?" Freedom asked with a worried look on her face.

"That's right, Freedom," I said. "It becomes real, doesn't it, when you actually see it happening with your own eyes? It's a shame to see this noble and great town destroyed."

Cam couldn't resist and got up to peer over the wall. "Oh man, this is crazy! There are a bunch of smaller boats getting closer to the shore."

"Yes, those smaller boats are carrying British soldiers from the bigger boats so that they can start to climb the hill," I said.

"Um, maybe we should think about our departure plan?" Liberty asked.

"This is going to be a blowout, isn't it?" Cam said. "I mean these American soldiers look completely tired and those British guys are marching this way like it's a school parade." He watched the sea of red starting to come up from the shore to the fort.

"A parade? Now you've made me curious," Freedom said, slowly standing up to look over the wall.

At the opposite side of the fort, a flash of white caught my eye. It seemed to come out of nowhere. I focused and saw an extraordinarily well-dressed man, unlike everyone else in the fort. The sun sparkled on his clothes, completely opposite to the dirty and hot surroundings. His face looked extremely calm.

"Dr. Warren?" I said, louder than I intended. "Wait, what is Dr. Warren doing here?" Freedom asked with the same concerned tone she had when the first cannon went off.

"I will go find out," I said. "Liberty, please keep Cam and Freedom here. I know you'll keep them safe," I said firmly. "I doubt we'll be able to stay here much longer so be ready to leave when I give the order."

"You got it, understood," said Liberty.

Immediately I ran toward the other end of the fort. "Dr. Warren, you probably don't remember, but I was at your home in Boston a while back with my students. You were kind enough to take us in and care for my student's illness," I said.

"Yes, of course, hello, Rush Revere!" Dr. Warren said, putting out his hand to shake mine. "How is Cam feeling?" He was such a personable and friendly man no matter the circumstance. I couldn't believe that in the midst of this battle he remembered our names.

"Cam feels much better now. In fact he is over there behind the wall with Freedom," I said. "Are you here to treat the injured soldiers?"

Dr. Warren kindly replied, "I am always willing to give medical assistance. But that is not my main purpose here. I have come to join these men and fight for freedom."

"Incredible," I said, almost to myself.

Dr. Warren gave a gentle smile. But there was something behind his eyes, too, a strength that was unmistakable. He turned and began to speak with the Patriots in the fort. Men gathered around him as if he were the head coach. I had not realized before now that Dr. Warren was both a well-known doctor in Boston, caring for patients, and a frontline fighter in the war.

"They're coming!" a voice shouted from somewhere inside the fort.

I could feel my heart beating with urgency. You could see the massive parade of Redcoats climbing steadily up the hill toward the fort.

Dr. Warren did all he could to boost the morale of the militia. "Be patient. Don't shoot until they are closer." His words drifted down the front line of men who were anxiously waiting to fire their guns.

"Don't shoot until you see the whites of their eyes!" a young soldier shouted.

Another said, "Yes, hold your ammunition, wait until you can see them clearly."

I knew the Americans were low on ammunition and couldn't hold off this attack for long. I stood frozen-still.

Dr. Warren shook me from my thoughts as he yelled, "Remember, we are fighting for our freedom!" He stood tall as he continued to move up and down the front of the fort, patting men on the back and encouraging them. The Redcoats were now close enough that I could see the silver on their buckles.

"Boom!" The exploding shot shocked my senses and I nearly jumped out of my boots. All the Patriot soldiers were pointing their guns downward at the British.

"Stay down, Mr. Revere," Dr. Warren said. "You are going to be all right." My heart was racing and sweat was pouring from my forehead.

Volley after volley, the shots rang through my ears. All around in front and to the sides of the fort the British seemed to fall and then come forward again. A sea of red started to wash up all around the outside walls.

Dr. Warren grabbed me roughly by the sleeve of my coat and said sternly, "I want you to leave now with your students. It won't be long until the British overtake the fort."

"I won't leave without you," I said, afraid for him.

"You must," said Dr. Warren. "It is my job to stay and fight, and it is your purpose to protect those children and share what happened here. We have showed the mighty British army that Patriots will fight. Go now!" Dr. Warren's eyes looked like they were on fire. He rushed back and I saw him disappear into the smoke and chaos.

"Mr. Revere!" Freedom shouted. She and Cam were already on top of Liberty.

I ran toward them and yelled, "Go, go, go!" as we ran from the battle. Gunshots rang out behind us. The back of the fort had caved in slightly, presumably from cannon fire. I looked quickly back as the Redcoats climbed over the unprotected walls and filled the overwhelmed fort.

Liberty raced ahead and I followed as quickly as humanly possible. I was exhausted by the time I met up with them under a large solitary tree, far from the battle.

Within the hour, several American soldiers hurried and stumbled before us, collapsing in the shade of our tree. Some had weapons and some did not. Some had shoes and some did not. Some had frontier clothing while others wore vests and coats reflective of city life.

A man who looked around thirty years old, with sweat and dirt smeared across his face, collapsed in the shade beside us. He still carried a sword. His leg was cut.

Freedom watched with tender eyes at his wound as the soldier ripped the hem of his shirt and used it to bandage his leg. Finally, he exhaled deeply and leaned back against the gnarled tree trunk.

"I will fight on," the worn-down soldier said, out of breath.

"How long have you been fighting?" asked Cam. The soldier slowly turned his head to see Cam on his other side.

"I stopped counting, friend. I'm not sure anymore, but not long enough. We must fight until we have our freedom," he said.

"Do you miss your family?" asked Cam.

"Yes, every single day. I wake up thinking of my son and how his mother is all alone. But I can't give up, it is for their future." The soldier closed his eyes for a moment.

This is a famous painting of the Battle of Bunker Hill. The Americans did not fire until the British were extremely close,

in order to conserve their limited ammunition. They said,
"Don't shoot until you see the whites of their eyes!"

Cam moved closer and said softly, "My dad is in the military, too, just like you. I don't really get to see him much."

"War is hard on everyone, both for the soldier and the ones they leave behind. Even though supplies are low, and we face hunger almost every day, with little to no weapons or gunpowder, we must never lose faith. We must never give up. We must fight for our freedom," said the soldier.

After all the excitement, I almost forgot the original reason we came here. I reached into my pocket and handed this soldier the inspirational note sent by George Washington.

"What's this?" he asked as he wiped his brow.

"I was asked by George Washington, the new Commander in Chief of the American army, to deliver this message for you to read and share with your captain and others."

The soldier seemed overwhelmed with emotion. "This is really from General Washington? I just can't believe this. This is incredible, thank you."

"We won't give up, either," said Cam.

"And we will fight like fathers who want desperately to return to their sons," the soldier said, winking at Cam. He pushed himself from the tree and began hobbling back toward Cambridge. "I must be on my way now. I must meet up with the rest of our men. Thank you, again!"

"We are proud of you!" Freedom said loud enough for him to hear.

We sat there for several more minutes before Liberty's stomach finally broke the silence as it rumbled like distant thunder.

"What do you say we get a little fuel in the tank, if you know what I mean?" asked Liberty.

"Excellent idea," I replied. "I think it's time we travel home. I know how grouchy you get when you're hungry." I winked.

"Grouchy?" asked Liberty. "I prefer to call it 'anxiously engaged' or 'persistently focused.' But if *grouchy* gets us home sooner, then I'm good with that, too."

Cam and Freedom climbed up onto Liberty and all he needed to say was, "*Rush, rush, rushing from history.*"

We landed back in the schoolyard at Manchester Middle School. As we were walking back toward the school entrance, Liberty for once was not thinking about snacks. He said, "You know, it's really amazing to think what's happened since the Pilgrims first arrived on the *Mayflower*. Actually, I should probably say it's amazing all we've seen since the Pilgrims and the *Mayflower*. I thought we were crazy to time-travel to the middle of the ocean on a small ship, but we've had a lot more crazy adventures since then!"

"Yeah, like being shot at?" Cam said with a laugh.

"Against my better judgment, I have to agree with Liberty again! It is truly amazing to think about what started with the Pilgrims and what made us into the country that we are today in just a few hundred years," I said, smiling.

"Cam, note that one in the compliment bank, too, will you?" Liberty winked.

"I got you!" Cam said, patting Liberty on the back.

"Why don't we meet in our usual spot on the field near the track tomorrow morning at nine o'clock?" I said.

Freedom sighed, "Okay, Mr. Revere, but can we go someplace less dangerous?"

Cam practically snorted. "I doubt Liberty can get us to the land of lollipops and unicorns."

"Is that a challenge?" asked Liberty. "Because I love a good challenge."

"Okay, you're on," said Cam. "And when you lose I get to ride you to school for a whole week."

"Well, when *you* lose," said Liberty, "you have to get me a week's supply of fresh vegetables *and* text every friend in your phone that you believe in unicorns."

Cam rolled his eyes and said, "Liberty, you're not going to win. Unicorns don't even exist."

"All right you two," I interrupted. "Enough bickering. Let's have a little peace, huh?"

"Pizza! Did you say pizza? I thought you'd never ask," blurted Liberty. "I'll take two large vegetarian pizzas, thank you."

We all laughed.

"Sounds like a good idea," I said.

"And I'll make sure Tommy comes tomorrow," Cam said, "if he isn't too busy scrapbooking."

A few minutes after 9 A.M. the next day, Tommy, Cam, and Freedom arrived together. Seeing all three of them made me realize they all wouldn't fit on one horse. Then again, perhaps we wouldn't need to travel anywhere once we arrived in 1775. Hmm, but what if we needed to make a daring escape? Better safe than sorry, I thought.

I whispered an idea into Liberty's ear and watched his face turn from a smile into a sour look.

Liberty whispered back, "You seriously want me to go and find Little Liberty?"

I nodded. "Hopefully, he stayed in Lexington, where we left him. You might try there first. Anyway, I want you to tell him to find his way to Cambridge and meet us there. Plus I think the kids would be thrilled to see their friend, again. It would be a fun surprise for them."

"Okay, fine. I'll do it for the kids. But it will cost you extra," Liberty said out loud.

While the students were talking I reached into Liberty's bag and fed him a giant, juicy apple.

"That's a start," he said and started chewing as he turned and exited the classroom.

I turned my back to Liberty and faced the kids. "Okay, guys, Liberty has to go take care of an errand. But he should be back soon."

"Mr. Revere," said Freedom, "since we're waiting I want to show you something I've been working on. It's a painting."

Freedom unrolled a small canvas and turned it in our direction. It was a painting of the Old North Church as we saw it from the wharf in Boston. A man was holding two lanterns from the highest window just below the tall white steeple.

"This is beautiful, Freedom," I said, and it really was.

"It's how I remember seeing it," Freedom said.

"Wow, it's great, Freedom. You really have a gift," Tommy added. "You should paint one of me rescuing Little Liberty at the Battle of Lexington!"

"I could try it," said Freedom, flattered.

"Ditto," said Cam. "You are way talented. Except Tommy's face might ruin the painting."

"Ha, ha," Tommy said as he slugged his best friend in the arm.

"Thanks, guys," said Freedom, shyly. "It's just a hobby, but I really enjoy painting."

"I think we should find a special place to hang your painting, Freedom," I said, beaming.

"I think we should hang it in our clubhouse," said Cam.

"We don't have a clubhouse," said Freedom.

"Well, our class is sort of our clubhouse," Cam said. "But we'll need a club name."

"How about the 'Jumping Spiders,'" said Tommy. "Seriously, jumping spiders are cool and they can leap to catch their prey just like we leap back in time."

"I vote no," said Freedom instantly. "No spiders. How about 'Spring Time Club'? Because we *spring* back in *time*. Get it?"

"I vote no," said Tommy. "No springy flower names."

"Oh brother, just because you're a boy you don't like flowers?" Freedom teased.

"I like flowers," Tommy said. "They attract insects and without insects I couldn't feed my spiders."

Cam raised his hand and said, "I have one. How about 'Rush Revere's Crew'?"

"Ooh, I like that!" Tommy said, giving Cam a high five.

"Yeah, me too!" Freedom added enthusiastically.

"Okay, everyone, huddle in! You, too, Mr. Revere," Cam said, motioning for all of us to put our hands in the center just like on the sideline of the dodgeball game. "Okay, ready, one, two, three . . . Rush Revere's Crew!" We all joined in.

Suddenly Liberty reentered the classroom.

"Hey there, welcome back!" I said. "Are we good?" I asked, trying not to give anything away.

"If by good you mean did I accomplish the mission of finding the little twerp, then yes, we are good," Liberty replied, rather annoyed.

"What twerp?" said Freedom, overhearing Liberty's reply.

"We have a special friend who will be joining us in our next time travel!" I said happily.

Liberty added, "He's a four-legged friend who's waiting for us in 1775." Liberty winked at Tommy.

"No way!" Tommy exclaimed. "Is it Little Liberty?"

"That's right," I said. "Earlier this morning, I asked Liberty to try to track down Little Liberty."

"It was easy," said Liberty. "The little pipsqueak was in a stable in Lexington. When he saw me he was really happy. Anyway, I helped him out of the stable and told him to meet all of us in Cambridge. It's only about ten miles from Lexington and he knows his way around those parts. He acted really excited to see Tommy."

"Can Little Liberty be part of Rush Revere's Crew?" Freedom asked with a smile.

"Absolutely not! Wait, what is Rush Revere's Crew?" Liberty asked.

"It's a long story, but yes, Freedom, I am going to overrule Liberty on this one," I said. "Both Liberty and Little Liberty are now officially part of Rush Revere's Crew!" We'd better get going, I thought; we don't want Little Liberty to beat us to Cambridge.

"So what's the game plan, Mr. Revere?" asked Cam.

"As you know, George Washington was appointed at the Second Continental Congress to lead the first official American army. Washington faced many problems when he became the leader of the army. He told you some of them, Cam, remember?"

"Yes, like his men weren't well trained and he didn't have as many guys as the British army and he didn't have money for supplies," Cam replied.

"Absolutely right, those are all very true," I continued. "But one of the biggest obstacles George Washington faced when he first became the leader was weapons. It's important to note that in 1775 the British Empire had the strongest fighting force in the world, including the army and navy. You can't beat the most powerful military in the world without weapons."

"What did Washington do?" Tommy asked. "I mean he can't just walk into a weapons depot and say, hey, I need some grenades to help out my army."

"No," I said, laughing. "An easy-access weapons depot wasn't an option, but Fort Ticonderoga was!"

"Oh no, are we going to another fort?" Freedom worried.

"No, don't worry, we won't be dodging any cannonballs this time! We are going to talk to George Washington and see how he went about getting more weapons for his army."

"Okay, that sounds cool," said Cam.

"Let's get going, Rush Revere's Crew," I said, delighted with the club's name. "Little Liberty is waiting."

We went outside to our usual spot, where Tommy and Freedom climbed onto Liberty's saddle. Cam and I followed close behind as Liberty said, *"Rush, rush, rushing to history."*

I yelled, "Cambridge, Massachusetts, November 1775!"

We jumped through the time portal and landed between a tall hedge and a large two-story home. Everything around us seemed to be brick and cobblestones. No rushing traffic or honking horns, just some chickens, goats, and carriages clacking past. As we walked around to the front of the home I saw beautiful big windows, including attic windows near the roof. There were two large brick chimneys on top.

"That house looks ginormous," said Tommy.

"Yeah, kinda like my house . . . ummmm, not so much," added Cam.

Liberty cleared his throat and said, "As your time-travel tour guide I can offer you a bit of fun trivia."

After a moment of silence I asked, "Let me guess, this bit of fun trivia isn't free."

"Hey, a time-traveling horse has to make a living somehow," Liberty quipped.

I reached into Liberty's saddlebag and pulled out a single sugar cube. I looked at the kids, who were all smiles. I said, "Let's see if this was worth it, shall we?" I fed the cube to Liberty.

"Yummy," said Liberty as he sucked on the cube. "That's why you're my favorite customers."

"I'm pretty sure we're your only customers. And we're all waiting for you to bless us with your knowledge of history," I teased.

"This is the headquarters for the Continental Army! General George Washington lives here," Liberty said proudly.

Suddenly, I heard a high-pitched whinny come from behind us. Running and pouncing, Little Liberty made a beeline toward the five of us. He nearly bowled Tommy over but instead, the pony rubbed up against his back and waist like an affectionate cat.

"Hey, Little Liberty," said Tommy. "I missed you, too!" He petted the pony with fondness. "He must still remember me saving him from the burning stables at Lexington."

"Oh, that's adorable. I love Little Liberty!" said Freedom as she watched the happy reunion.

"It's a toss-up between adorable and annoying. I can't make up my mind," Liberty jabbed.

"Well, Liberty," I said, "maybe spending more time with Little Liberty will help you decide. The rest of us are going to visit with George Washington. We'll come back outside as soon as we can."

"Oh, joy," said Liberty with sarcasm. "I get to babysit the Oompah-Loompah."

I was the first on the porch and quickly rapped on the door.

A man in a military uniform opened the door. I assumed he was a member of George Washington's staff. "Do you have an appointment?" asked the man.

Before I could respond, George Washington appeared from a back room sorting through several pages of notes or maybe maps. As soon as he saw me he said, "Mr. Revere, glad you are back. I was just about to visit with my troops. Come walk with me and tell me your experience at Bunker Hill." He walked like a true military man and he seemed even taller than before. Perhaps it was simply the idea that he was in charge of all of America's military. He stepped outside and I quickly kept stride with him as the kids followed.

"Mr. Revere, look all around you: this is the new Continental Army camp," General Washington said.

I noticed many tents set up in the spacious yard. There were lots of men roaming around doing different things. Some were sitting in a circle cooking while smoke rose around them; others were laughing, some more serious. Most of the men did not have uniforms and were dressed in all sorts of regional clothing.

"I expect to have twenty thousand willing soldiers here soon. More men are coming every day and God willing, we will prevail," General Washington said as he continued our tour.

"Are they going to build forts?" Tommy asked. He must have been talking to Cam about Bunker Hill.

"Yes, I suppose they will in time. However, the men must learn how to build forts and really anything involved with battles," General Washington replied. "Most have never fought before, nor do they have the first clue about discipline or what it means to be a part of a single army. Nevertheless, they have left their former lives behind and are here willing to fight for our lives and our freedom."

Cam smiled and replied, "If anyone can get them to listen, it's you. Even now I can see how your men admire you. They clear the path and straighten up when you walk by. I think they believe in you."

"Thank you, Cameron," said Washington. "Having the belief to win is an important part of my strategy. Equally important is getting these men to work together in one unified effort. If I can get them all doing the same thing at the right time, we may have a chance to win this war."

I turned to Cam and said, "Sounds like the same strategy you used to beat Billy."

"True," Cam said. "I know what it's like to have a team that's totally disorganized and outnumbered. But I also know that learning to work as a team makes all the difference."

George smiled. "It sounds like your team believed in you, too."

"Yeah, I guess they did," Cam replied.

"What are you doing to gather weapons and supplies?" I asked the General, knowing that was a weakness Washington had to overcome. I assumed he had a plan in place.

"That is something I am working on day in and day out," Washington said. "We received funding from some wealthy Patriot merchants, and Congress gave some funding as well. But it is not enough. We need guns and cannons now, before it is too late."

Liberty pushed his nose in between Washington and me as if to say, *Remember me? The horse that got you here?*

George smiled and touched his hand to Liberty's nose and noted, "You have a magnificent horse. He looks strong and smart."

I thought to myself, If you mean *smart aleck*, yes, he is. Smiling, I replied, "He's been a faithful companion and a true Patriot."

George raised an eyebrow and asked, "Perhaps you'd be willing to enlist him in the Continental Army? I'm looking for a good horse. Riding a true Patriot into war could make all the difference."

Liberty's eyes went wide.

Giving up Liberty to help George Washington wasn't an option, or was it? I didn't expect what happened next. Then again, with Liberty everything was unexpected.

Chapter 9

Suddenly, *Liberty's legs* buckled and he fainted, falling straight to the ground. He looked like he was completely out cold!

"Liberty? Liberty! Are you okay?" Freedom cried, running over to kneel beside him.

Liberty was on his side with both eyes shut. I wondered if this was one of his attention-seeking stunts. I took a deep breath and tried to explain the situation. "Don't worry, General Washington, please go on ahead. My horse was a little under the weather yesterday and probably just needs a little rest." Gratefully, Liberty didn't seem hurt, just fast asleep.

"All right, but please do let me know if there is anything our men can do to help. Poor fellow," Washington said, looking kindly at Liberty before walking back toward the house.

"I think he was really scared about the idea of being enlisted into the army!" Tommy said, chuckling.

"Yeah, I bet he passed out when he realized he wouldn't be getting six meals a day," Cam said with a laugh.

"You guys shouldn't be laughing," Freedom said in a soft voice as she patted Liberty's side. "Poor Liberty."

Liberty slowly opened one eye and weakly said, "No energy. Need carrot."

I was relieved that Liberty was waking up but I still wasn't totally sure if this was a stunt.

"I'll get one!" Tommy said, pulling a carrot from the saddlebag and waving it in front of Liberty's nose. "Liberty . . . wake up!" he added.

Liberty grabbed the carrot in his mouth and chomped it down.

"Why isn't he getting up?" Tommy asked.

"No energy. Need apple," said Liberty, like he was on his deathbed. He was coughing and wheezing.

"He sounds awful," said Cam as he reached for an apple and fed it to Liberty.

Liberty chomped the juicy apple with his eyes closed. "Maybe one more carrot. And a sugar cube would be nice."

Freedom gave Liberty a big hug and said, "I'm glad you are awake and feeling better!"

"Okay, up and at 'em!" I said to Liberty. If he had truly fainted he was clearly recovered now. I couldn't help but smile at him despite myself. "It looks as though General Washington has had second thoughts about recruiting Liberty as his warhorse."

"Whewww," Liberty said under his breath but loud enough for us to hear.

"Hey, where's Little Liberty?" asked Tommy.

"He was with us when George Washington was here," said Freedom.

"Liberty, do you sense him?" I asked.

"It feels like he's nearby, yes," said Liberty. "I think he was hungry and went looking for something to eat."

"I'll need some volunteers to track down Little Liberty," I said.

"Not me," said Tommy. "I'm sticking with you like glue, Mr. Revere."

Apparently, the incident at the Battle of Lexington had left a lasting impression on Tommy.

"I'll go," said Cam. "Since this whole area is the Continental Army headquarters I doubt we'll run into any Redcoats."

"True," I said, "but under no circumstances should you leave Liberty."

"I'll stick with Liberty, too," said Freedom. She climbed onto Liberty's saddle with Cam.

Liberty looked very content with the decision.

"Fair enough," I said. "Once you find Little Liberty bring him back here."

"You got it, Captain," said Liberty. "Let's go, troops!"

As we parted ways, Tommy said, "I never got a chance to talk with George Washington. I saw him at the First Continental Congress but he was with a lot of the other delegates."

"Then I'm glad you chose to stick with me," I said. "And you can help me explain what we learn to Cam and Freedom later."

We walked back to the Continental Army headquarters, passing a guard to enter the home. As we walked through the doorway I noticed several senior military officers seated in ornate chairs in the large front room.

"How is your horse, Mr. Revere?" General Washington asked as he looked up from a large map on the table.

"He is much better, thank you. My other students are caring for him," I replied. Just as I was about to ask about the map he was studying, a uniformed soldier briskly approached the General and said, "Sir, I apologize for interrupting, but Henry Knox says he has urgent news and wishes to speak with you immediately."

"Please send him in," General Washington said in a pleasant but firm tone.

In seconds, a large man came bounding down the hallway and right up to the General. He reminded me of Ed, talking excitedly about the plan to defeat Billy's team. Henry Knox had chubby red cheeks and wore a big smile. His uniform looked a little small.

Before General Washington had a chance to make introductions, Knox blurted out, "I have a plan to get the cannons. I know it will work. I know how to do it!" He was full of excitement.

The two other officers in the room did not share the same enthusiasm. Honestly, they looked like they had too much starch in their shorts.

Washington held up his hand to calm Knox. He turned to me and said, "Rush Revere, meet Henry Knox. Henry has proven himself a true Patriot in the past several years. He is young and tireless. And I like the way he thinks." General Washington didn't smile but his eyes twinkled as he glanced at Knox. He continued: "Henry has a brilliant mind and I've been impressed with the fortifications he designed near Roxbury."

"Thank you, sir," said Knox.

"And this is Rush Revere. He is a friend and a Son of Liberty. He and I first met at the First Continental Congress. Samuel

Adams and John Hancock told me that he risked his life in helping Paul Revere warn of the Redcoat invasion at Lexington and
Concord." General Washington gestured to Tommy. "And this
young man is one of his students."

"It is a pleasure meeting you, Mr. Knox," I said, smiling.

General Washington turned to Henry and asked, "Now then,
how are you coming with the artillery?"

Knox nearly jumped from his mud-crusted boots and said,
"I have wonderful news! This morning when I examined the
map an idea struck me on how to retrieve the guns. Let me show
you." He moved across the room like a bull in a china shop. Several vases nearly toppled to the floor by the time he reached the
center table. He unfolded a large parchment and placed it on
the table so everyone could see. As he smoothed out the corners
I noticed it was a map of the New England states and eastern
New York State. "Here!" cheered Knox. He pointed a chubby
finger at New York, specifically at the southern end of Lake
Champlain, at a place called Fort Ticonderoga. He practically
screamed, "We can get them from Ticonderoga!"

Tommy whispered, "Hey, Ticonderoga! I remember you
said it's the next-best thing to a weapons depot, right?" Tommy
smirked.

I nodded, impressed with Tommy's memory.

Frowning, an older military man who was missing a finger
said, "General Washington, this plan is outrageous. Ticonderoga
is nearly three hundred miles away, through harsh terrain. It will
take months and thousands of men to bring those guns back
here. It is a fool's journey to—"

Washington calmly interrupted: "I am interested to hear what
Knox has to say." He nodded for Henry to continue.

This is Colonel Henry Knox. Does he look like what you imagined?

"Sir, we can do it," Henry said with confidence, still smiling. "I hope to bring back up to sixty heavy cannons down Lake George and the Hudson River to Albany, then pull them across Massachusetts."

The military officer was laughing now and shaking his head. "An absolute impossibility," he said.

"I concur," said the other officer in the room, who had the shiniest boots I had ever seen. "The idea is utter nonsense. These cannons weigh up to three thousand pounds, some heavier."

"Wow!" exclaimed Tommy. "Don't even ask UPS to deliver something that heavy."

"Who is UPS? Are those someone's initials?" Washington asked.

Everyone stared at Tommy. Would he tell them the real meaning was United Parcel Service?

Tommy slowly replied, "Oh, um, yeah. UPS stands for . . ." He paused. But his thoughtful expression soon changed to a smile. "It stands for Unusually Powerful Storm-troopers."

"Storm troopers?" asked Washington. "I have never heard of these troops."

Tommy nodded. "Well, yeah. These troops specialize in delivering the mail, especially in storms." Tommy looked my way and gave me an awkward grin.

"I see," said George. "I may need to use these Unusually Powerful Storm-troopers someday. Now then, if no one else has a better plan, I'm inclined to support the mission to Ticonderoga."

The senior officer with a missing finger replied, "Sir, this is ridiculous, and a waste of time. We should concentrate our limited energies elsewhere."

Ignoring the officer, General Washington stood with authority and said, "I have seen what Knox has done with our fortifications. He is loyal. He is smart. He is fearless. He witnessed the Boston Massacre and fought at the Battle of Bunker Hill. I have seen him take on challenge after challenge and rise to every occasion."

The officer with the shiny boots was turning red. "But, sir, he is only twenty-five years old, not to mention he is overweight. And just look at the mud on his boots."

Knox shifted in his muddy boots as he listened to the debate.

"He may be young, but these colonies are young. He may have mud on his boots, but we could all use a little mud once in a while," said General Washington.

Exasperated, the older officer replied, "Yes, but this shows a lack of discipline. We will never win against the King's Empire with disorderly conduct and delirious ideas. I strongly object to this plan, sir!"

The fire crackled and popped in the fireplace. Nobody in the room dared to move or say a word until George Washington broke the silence.

"Your objection is noted. Thank you," said Washington. "But I believe we need more men like Henry Knox. Or should I say Colonel Knox of the Continental Army."

Knox beamed at the promotion and bowed slightly to his commander in chief. "I will do you and this country right, sir," said Knox. "See you soon with the guns of Ticonderoga."

"Our freedom depends on it," said General Washington.

Without another word, Colonel Knox gathered his map and bounded out the door, leaving a trail of dried mud. Even after he was outside I could hear his voice yelling for men to gather

Can you guess the name of this fort? Hint—Henry Knox took the fort's guns back to George Washington in Boston. It is Fort Ticonderoga. Henry Knox brought back these cannons hundreds of miles through the snow.

supplies. The other military leaders looked upset as they left the room and exited the house.

I glanced through the window and noticed Liberty and Freedom arriving with Cam and Little Liberty trailing close behind. It seemed like a good time to say our goodbyes and be off.

"Thank you, General Washington," I said, putting out my hand to shake his. "This has been most informative. I look forward to our next visit."

"I hope Colonel Knox gets the cannons!" Tommy said with a smile as we walked toward the door.

"So do I," George Washington said. "If Knox manages to get those guns from Fort Ticonderoga we have a fighting chance to win this war."

Once again we said our goodbyes and walked out to the porch and over to where the rest of Rush Revere's Crew had gathered.

Tommy raced up to Little Liberty and petted his bushy head. "I'm glad they found you," said Tommy. "Where was he?"

"In someone's garden making himself a snack," said Liberty. "Seriously, this kid needs a babysitter twenty-four/seven." Liberty leaned close to my ear and whispered, "We're leaving the pony here, right? Please tell me we're leaving him here."

I temporarily ignored Liberty and said, "We need to find a secluded place to time-jump. It looks like there's a small pasture beyond those trees. Tommy, you should tell the rest of our Crew what happened inside."

"Oh, yeah! They were having this top-secret meeting about getting guns from Fort Ticonderoga to fight the British."

Cam perked up and jokingly asked, "Top secret? Was super-spy James Bond there? Oh, wait, isn't James Bond British?"

"It wasn't Double-O Seven. But he was big enough to be Triple-O Seven. Seriously, this dude was big."

I clarified: "His name is Henry Knox."

"Yeah, that's right. Henry Knox was taking on this grumpy older guy who was getting mad for trying to get the weapons. But George Washington was totally on Knox's side," Tommy said.

Cam and Freedom stayed on Liberty and Tommy rode Little Liberty. As we walked, Tommy filled in the details of the Ticonderoga conversation. When he finished, he asked, "So, what are we going to do with Little Liberty?"

"I say let's feed him a Pop Tart and send him on his way!" blurted Liberty. "Seriously! You can't hear him talking but I can. He's inside my head. He doesn't stop asking questions. I feel like I've been trapped inside a horsey day care with hundreds of foals asking me hundreds of questions. It's driving me bonkers!"

"What kinds of questions is he asking?" Freedom asked.

"Oh, things like 'What do you do if you see an endangered animal eating an endangered plant? If a cow laughed would milk come out of its nose? After eating, do amphibians have to wait an hour before getting out of the water?'"

Tommy and Cam started laughing. Even Freedom was smiling.

I interrupted and said, "Okay, we get it. Look, just tell Little Liberty to trot back to the stable that you got him from. Tell him you'll come back later and bring him a bunch of carrots."

As Liberty paused to telepathically communicate the message, Tommy dismounted and patted his fuzzy friend one last time. Then Little Liberty swished his tail and darted off down the road toward Lexington.

"Bye-bye, Little Liberty!" yelled Tommy.

"Well, that's a relief," Liberty sighed.

"Now, let's get home," I said.

"All aboard the Manchester Middle School Express," said Liberty. "*Rush, rush, rushing from history.*"

Liberty leapt through the portal and Tommy and I followed close behind.

The following morning was July Fourth. I had planned to postpone our class until after the holiday but Cam, Tommy, and Freedom all said they wanted to attend as long as we had it in the morning. It was nine o'clock when Freedom and Tommy walked into the history classroom.

"Where's Liberty?" asked Freedom.

"I sent him to check up on Little Liberty. I wanted to be sure he made it back to Lexington."

I noticed Cam was late, which was odd for him.

"Have you talked to Cam?" I asked.

"Not this morning," Freedom replied.

"Me, neither," said Tommy. "I'll text him."

"Thank you, Tommy. You know it's too bad our American team during the Revolutionary War didn't have the ability to text. I mean, we can send a message in a matter of seconds. But the colonies and Patriots in 1775 didn't have cell phones. Do you know what they used to send a message?"

"Snail mail," said Tommy.

"Yeah, they had to use paper to write letters and notes," said Freedom.

"And we know they used messengers like Paul Revere," said Tommy.

COMMON SENSE;

ADDRESSED TO THE *W. Hamilton*

INHABITANTS

OF

AMERICA,

On the following interesting

SUBJECTS.

I. Of the Origin and Design of Government in general, with concise Remarks on the English Constitution.

II. Of Monarchy and Hereditary Succession.

III. Thoughts on the present State of American Affairs.

IV. Of the present Ability of America, with some miscellaneous Reflections.

by Thomas Paine

Man knows no Master save creating HEAVEN,
Or those whom choice and common good ordain.
THOMSON.

PHILADELPHIA;
Printed, and Sold, by R. BELL, in Third-Street.
MDCCLXXVI.

Common Sense is the pamphlet written by Thomas Paine that inspired people in the thirteen colonies to declare and fight for independence from Great Britain in the Summer of 1776.

This is Thomas Paine, author of *Common Sense*.
He met Benjamin Franklin in London, England, in 1772.

"Very good," I nodded.

"And I remember they printed newspapers," said Tommy. "Benjamin Franklin owned a printing press."

"True," I said. "There were many printers in the colonies. In fact, there was a very important pamphlet written by the patriot Thomas Paine called *Common Sense*. It was like a newspaper and was written in very plain language for the everyday person in America. It was the first published work to openly ask for independence from Great Britain."

"So, everyday language like—'What's up, bro? Let's get some freedom y'all'?" Tommy joked.

"Kind of," I said. "At that time, language could be really complicated and the issues were really difficult. Paine made really complex things easy to understand. That was Thomas Paine's genius—the way he made everyone understand exactly what they were fighting for." I went on, "In fact, George Washington was so inspired by Paine's words that he read the *Common Sense* pamphlet to his troops in one of their worst moments, when they thought they were going to lose the war. General Washington wanted them to know that in the most difficult times their characters are tested the most. Listen to these words and tell me if you know what they mean."

> *These are the times that try men's souls. The summer soldier and the sunshine patriot will, in the crisis, shrink from the service of their country.*

I was afraid the words were a little over their heads so I was surprised when Freedom raised her hand and said, "I think I know what it means. War is really hard, not like the fun of the summer."

"Absolutely right, Freedom. Great answer!" I said, thrilled, and launched into a full explanation. "In addition to that, it means that soldiers stuck in the hardest times of war must dig deep into their souls to keep fighting for their country even when they think they are ready to give up. Thomas Paine wrote in 1775 and 1776 during a very difficult time for the American Patriots. People were so inspired by his writing and arguments that they bought hundreds of thousands of copies in all thirteen colonies. That's an amazing number of copies to sell during that time in history!" I exclaimed.

"I bet people read it because it was short," said Tommy, joking.

"Yeah, Tommy likes short books like *The Cat in the Hat*," teased Freedom.

We all laughed. "Ha, ha," said Tommy. "In all seriousness, this Thomas Paine guy sounds like he really got the word out. It sounds like something Samuel Adams would've done, right? He was really good at getting people fired up against the British, too."

"You are exactly right, Tommy. Both Thomas Paine and Samuel Adams were early American Patriots and both had a similar mission to rally the people of the thirteen colonies so that they would fight back against the British."

The door opened and Cam walked in. He said, "Sorry I'm late. It's a long a story." Someone else followed him into the class.

"Hello, Ed," I said. "Welcome to our summertime history class." I was not expecting another student and wondered why Cam had brought him.

Before Cam took a seat he walked by me and whispered, "Ed was having a rough day. I think Billy had been picking on him. So I invited him to class. I hope that's okay."

"No problem. We'll make it work," I replied softly.

Ed was carrying an instrument case, maybe a flute or clarinet, and seemed genuinely excited to see his friends from the dodge-ball team. "Hi, Mr. Revere. I didn't know there was a summer school course for American history. It was the best news I've heard all summer. Cam said I could come if I wanted to."

"Any friend of Cam's is a friend of mine," I said, smiling. "You're always welcome," I added. Unless we have to time-travel, I thought. Hmm, we might have to postpone our field trip.

"Where's Liberty?" asked Cam.

"Who's Liberty?" Ed questioned.

"Oh, um, he's a horse, but he's special," said Cam, looking over at Ed. "You could say he's our class mascot."

Ed looked a little surprised. "You mean a *real* horse? Inside the classroom?"

"Yep," said Cam.

"Uh-oh," said Ed. "I'm allergic to horses."

"Good to know," I said. "Freedom, you might want to *send a note* to Liberty about that if you know what I mean." I winked, hoping she understood that I needed her to speak to Liberty's mind before he returned to the classroom.

"Oh, okay, no problem, Mr. Revere," replied Freedom.

"Your horse can read notes?" Ed asked skeptically.

"Uh, yes, sort of," I said, not sure how much I wanted to reveal to Ed. "Anyway, Liberty is running an errand for me so he'll be a little late."

"You send your horse on errands?" asked Ed, confused.

"He's a specially trained horse, like a Seeing Eye dog," said Cam, like it was perfectly normal.

I tried to change the subject. "I think with the arrival of our friend Ed we're going to play a game and split you into teams today. Since Ed hasn't been with us for our previous lessons and field trips I think that's only fair."

"Uh-oh, this class goes on field trips?" asked Ed. "I'm allergic to buses."

"Good to know," I said.

"I should probably give you this," said Ed. "It's a list of all the things I'm allergic to." Ed handed me a small notebook. "It's categorized alphabetically." He smiled.

"Again, good to know," I repeated, thumbing through the pages. "Now then, let's have Freedom and Tommy against Cam and Ed. We'll see how that works. We can always change things up later."

"What game are we playing again, Mr. Revere?" Tommy asked.

"It's a quiz game. I'm going to ask you some questions about American history. Each team will take turns. If your team doesn't know the answer to a question, the other team gets a chance to answer it and steal your points. Got it?"

The students all nodded.

"Good, then let's jump in," I said. "We'll start with Cam and Ed. Question number one. Who was the leader of the first American army—the Continental Army—and how did he get the job?"

Freedom jumped in: "I hope our question is as easy as that one."

Cam smiled and said, "We'll take it! Our answer is George Washington and he was made commander in chief of the army at the Second Continental Congress."

"One point to Cam and Ed, that is exactly right. Okay, next question goes to Tommy and Freedom," I said.

"What was the name of the man in the Continental Army

who had the ingenious plan to travel to Fort Ticonderoga to retrieve artillery for General Washington? Was it a) Henry Fox, b) Henry Clocks, c) Henry Knox, or d) Henry Litterbox?"

Tommy's hand shot up into the air. "It was c) Henry Knox. How could I forget him? I wish we had more time to talk to him. He seemed cool."

"Spot-on, you got it, point to Tommy and Freedom's team," I said, thrilled that these answers came so easily to them. "After Knox got the approval from General Washington in November, Knox and a group of others set out for Lake Champlain, and they got to Fort Ticonderoga on December fifth. It took fifty-one days to travel three hundred miles back to Boston. It is incredible that they made it!"

"Those questions were pretty easy, Mr. Revere," Cam said.

"Okay, this one is a toughie. Are you ready? Cam and Ed, how many cannons did Henry Knox bring back from Fort Ticonderoga to General Washington in Boston? Was it a) almost twenty pieces, b) almost thirty pieces, c) almost forty pieces, or d) almost sixty pieces?"

Cam and Ed started whispering to each other. Finally, Cam raised his hand and said, "Well, Ed wasn't there, of course, and I can't remember the exact number, but we know George Washington needed a lot of guns to get the British out of Boston. Ed wants me to say almost sixty pieces."

"Is that your final answer?" I asked.

"Yes," said Ed.

"Correct again," I said. "The exact number of weapons that Henry Knox brought back was fifty-nine. Keep in mind that was fifty-nine pieces of huge, heavy iron and brass cannons and mortars. Can you imagine trying to pull basically fifty-nine

cars through the snow for miles? It is absolutely amazing what they did."

"Come to think of it, how did Henry Knox pull all of those heavy weapons across the snow?" asked Tommy. "I mean he didn't really look like he was an Olympic athlete. He was more like a really cool Olympic couch potato." He smiled at his commentary.

"For the record, some of us large couch potatoes are really smart and we use our brains to solve the impossible," said Ed, sounding a little offended.

"I'm sorry, Ed. But I think you're really cool, too." Tommy said sheepishly.

"That's okay, Tommy, we're good." Ed tried to fist-bump Tommy but missed.

"That is an excellent question, Tommy," I said. "The Knox brothers actually used flatboats to float the weapons and artillery as far as they could down Lake George and the Hudson River. See, right here." I pointed to a large map on the board at the front of the class and ran my finger down the waterway to show the movement. "Once they got here, they used oxen and horses and sleds to pull the really heavy weapons, kind of like hauling a large boat out of the water at a lake. As you can imagine, it took a long time to travel the entire length of Massachusetts!"

Cam jumped in: "Yeah, no kidding! I don't think our crew could have brought one weapon back, never mind fifty-nine!"

Tommy flexed his arm muscles and said, "I'm not so sure. Have you seen these cannons?" We all laughed.

"If those are cannons, then America is in big trouble," teased Freedom.

"Ha, ha," said Tommy. "But seriously, what did General

Washington do when the Knox brothers got back with the weapons? I mean he was probably super-relieved. I mean you guys weren't there but these other military dudes totally laughed at how dumb Knox's idea was. They probably weren't laughing very much when Henry Knox made it back and saved the day!"

I explained that Tommy was entirely right. "General Washington was so impressed by Knox's huge accomplishment and was very relieved. If the Americans hadn't secured those weapons it is very likely they would have had no chance whatsoever and would have lost the war. Thankfully, the *impossible* mission was a success. This was a turning point for the American team. The Americans were able to surround the British army in Boston, by occupying a place called Dorchester Heights."

"Did you say Dork-chester?" asked Tommy, obviously trying to get a laugh.

"No," I said. "Dorchester Heights. It's located here," I added, pointing to the south side of Boston. "It's the highest area just south of Boston that has a view of both Boston Harbor and the city of Boston. The American team, or first Continental Army, used the big cannons and guns that Knox brought back."

Smiling, Freedom raised her hand and asked, "So just to be sure, you're referring to the *big* cannons, not Tommy's *little* cannons?"

"Ohhhhhh, ouch!" said Cam. "Freedom is dishing it out today."

Tommy smiled wide, "Okay, I see how it is. Just remember, someday you might need these cannons." Tommy flexed again, clearly teasing Freedom back.

She nodded and said, "Oh, really? I heard how those cannons really saved you in Lexington."

"Seriously?" Tommy cringed while laughing. "I am going to be haunted by the Battle of Lexington for the rest of my life."

Everyone was laughing now. I wished Liberty was here because he would be rolling on the floor.

I raised my hand to calm everyone down and said, "As I was saying, these big cannons from Ticonderoga could reach the water from the high location and scare the pants off the British army. In fact the British were so nervous and afraid when they saw the big cannons pointing down at them that they finally decided to retreat and leave Boston. George Washington and the Continental Army had done it. The American underdogs had won a vital early victory."

"That's way cool," Cam said, soaking up the American strategy. Ever since the dodgeball game you could see his wheels turning whenever strategy was discussed.

"Okay, here's a question for Tommy and Freedom: what did Thomas Paine write?"

"*Common Sense!*" they both said.

"Correct, again!" I said.

"Wow! You guys answered that fast," said Cam.

"We just learned it while you and Ed were coming to class," said Freedom.

Ed did some quick math and said, "We are tied, Mr. Revere. Both teams have answered two questions each."

Hmm, it was time to wrap things up. "Okay, since we are all tied up, this question will be *Jeopardy!*-style. The first person to buzz in with the right answer gets the winning point for their team," I said.

"When did the Americans first declare independence from Great Britain?"

Tommy slammed his hand down on the imaginary buzzer on his desk and shouted, "July Fourth, 1776!"

"Exactly right! Tommy and Freedom's team wins! You are the official winners," I cheered. Tommy got out from his seat and did a small victory lap around the room. Surprisingly, Cam and Ed were very good sports and gave him a high five when he rounded their chairs.

"Congrats!" Cam said.

"What do we win?" Freedom asked.

"You each win a special field trip to the place of your choice. You can choose from your favorite restaurant, your favorite movie theater, or the ice-skating rink," I replied.

"Oh, cool, thanks, Mr. Revere! I'll have to think about this," Freedom said with a big smile.

"Yeah, thanks!" said Tommy, smiling.

"And you can each bring a friend, too. I will give your parents a call and give them the details," I said.

"Awesome!" Freedom seemed genuinely thrilled. "Oh, by the way, Liberty is back," Freedom whispered.

"Does she mean your horse?" asked Ed. "She must have really good hearing. Hey, how does he get inside the school? Wait, don't tell me. He can open doors, too."

"No worries, Ed," I said. "He'll stay outside until class is dismissed."

Ed exhaled, looking a bit confused. "That's a relief because you do not want to see me break out in hives."

A car horn honked three times. Ed looked at his watch and said, "That's my mom. She's picking me up for band practice."

"You have band practice on a holiday?" I asked.

"Well, my mom is the band teacher," Ed said, grinning. "And

today I get to organize all of the instruments in the new storage cabinets we have. Thanks for inviting me, Cam. This is the most fun I've had in a class, ever." He gathered his bag and instrument case and scrambled out the door.

"I hope Ed doesn't run into Liberty in the hallway!" Cam said.

"He won't," said Freedom. "Liberty's waiting for us outside. He says he has a surprise for Cam."

"For me?" Cam asked. "Why me?"

Freedom smirked, "Oh, you'll see. He said it has something to do with a bet the two of you made with each other."

Cam's brow rose for a second as he thought about what it could be.

Chapter 10

*A*s we walked outside by the big oak tree it was apparent that Liberty had been busy. The entire schoolyard looked like it was growing with lollipops. Someone or, more accurately, some horse had stuck hundreds of small lollipops into the grass as if they were growing like multicolored dandelions. I'll admit, it was very impressive. Cam's jaw dropped when he saw the candied display. Suddenly Liberty appeared from the corner of the building as he galloped along a path through the lollipops.

"What's that on Liberty's head?" Tommy asked.

"No way," said Cam, laughing.

"It looks like a horn made out of a carrot," said Tommy. "Wait, is he supposed to be a unicorn? He realizes we wear costumes for Halloween not the Fourth of July, right?"

"He knows," said Freedom. "Cam bet Liberty that the Land of Lollipops and Unicorns didn't exist."

Cam took out his phone and took a picture of a smiling Liberty galloping by with an authentic-looking unicorn-horn carrot strapped to his head.

After Liberty's antics had ended, Cam agreed that Liberty pulled it off and chuckled as he posted an Instagram photo to all his friends with the caption, "Unicorns really do exist!"

"Let's meet by the large flagpole at the entrance of the school," I announced. "Since it's the Fourth of July, Liberty and I have something special planned."

We all gathered at the base of the flagpole. The crystal blue sky was the perfect backdrop for the large American flag that was gently waving in the summer breeze.

"I've asked Liberty to share something he memorized. See if you can guess what he is reciting."

Liberty looked around to make sure we were alone. Knowing that everyone was listening closely, he decided to make the most of it. Liberty cleared his throat, took a deep breath, and said in a booming voice, "We hold these truths to be self-evident, that all men are created equal, that they are endowed by their Creator, with certain unalienable Rights, that among these are Life, Liberty, and the pursuit of Happiness."

"Anyone want to take a guess where these words are from?" I asked.

"I bet it has something to do with the flag," said Freedom.

"Yeah, the flag or the Fourth of July," said Tommy.

Seeing another opportunity to perform, Liberty said, "Wait, wait, maybe you need for me to say it again, only this time with a little more passion, a little more heart. . . . Fear not, I have you covered!"

All three kids laughed at Liberty's dramatics.

"Liberty, please go ahead and recite the same part again," I urged.

"Well, if you insist," Liberty said. He took a deep breath and continued: "We hold these truths to be self-evident, that all men are created equal, that they are endowed by their Creator, with certain unalienable Rights, that among these are Life, Liberty, and the pursuit of Happiness."

Freedom clapped and said, "Good job, Liberty, you're the best!"

"Here's a hint," I said. "The Continental Congress adopted these words on July 4th, 1776."

"The Constitution?" Freedom asked.

"Very close, Freedom, but this one declared something . . ." I hinted.

Tommy smiled and confidently piped in, "I got it! It's the Declaration of Independence!"

"That's absolutely right," I said, smiling. "Well done, Tommy! To be exact, what Liberty recited is the Preamble, which means the introduction to the Declaration of Independence."

I explained that every year Americans celebrate the Fourth of July, almost like a birthday for the country, even though the actual independence of the United States of America came five years after the Declaration of Independence was signed in 1776.

Cam scratched his head and said, "So if we didn't actually win the war on the Fourth of July, why do we celebrate it every year? I mean there are lots of barbecues and fireworks and flags and stuff at the base. It's usually a big party. Everyone says 'Happy Independence Day!' So I always thought that meant it was our country's birthday."

"That is a very good observation, Cam. Patriots from the thirteen colonies declared their independence from Britain after the battles at Lexington, Concord, and Bunker Hill. They were drawing a line in the sand, basically saying enough is enough, we want to have our own free country with our own laws and rules. As you can imagine, after King George saw how prosperous the colonies had become from the time that the Pilgrims arrived, he was not eager to give up control of the land or the people. George Washington and his American army continued fighting for another five years, if you can imagine that, before there was actual independence."

Tommy raised his hand and said, "I think the Patriots were kinda telling King George to take a hike, right, Mr. Revere?"

"In a manner of speaking, yes," I said. "July Fourth is the day the Patriots officially listed all of the ways King George and the English government, or Parliament, mistreated the colonists and declared in writing that they wanted to be their own country. Essentially, it was the day the Patriots penned their breakup letter to the King of England."

"It was bound to happen," Liberty said. "Long-distance relationships are so hard."

"Ohhhhh, I get it," exclaimed Tommy. "The Declaration of Independence is sort of like when my older sister texted her boyfriend to say she was breaking up with him. He was not happy. I bet King George wasn't happy when he got our text."

Liberty chuckled. "Imagine if we swapped out the word *text* as in text message for the word *declaration*. *Hey, did you get my declaration? Yeah, I already declarationed you back. Well, I didn't get it so declaration me, again!*" The kids all laughed at Liberty's commentary.

I added, "Picture it this way. Since Tommy is a quarterback for the Manchester Lions, let's use him as an example. What if Tommy played quarterback for King George's British Empire team? What if the King benched Tommy and said he couldn't play anymore unless he played by the King's rules? But his rules made Tommy a robot. His rules forced Tommy to do anything the King wanted no matter what happened to Tommy or in the game. What if the rules were unfair and somehow hurt Tommy or his family? Would you just keep playing by those rules? Or would you eventually say, hey, enough is enough?"

"I'd say enough is enough," Tommy said.

Cam blurted, "Oh boy, if my mom found out that my coach was like that, she'd march right over to his house and give him a piece of her mind."

I smiled and said, "And that's exactly what America did. The Declaration of Independence was a piece of our mind to King George."

Cam smiled and said, "I would've loved to have been a fly on the wall when King George first received the Declaration of Independence." Cam put on his best King George British accent and said, "'Oh, look, a letter from America. Let's see what it says.'" Cam cleared his throat. "*Dear King George: We think you smell like rotten cheese, and we are not letting you bully us anymore!*"

Everyone laughed. I looked up at the clock and then out the window. Two cars pulled up, one right after the other, at the school bus drop-off area.

"It looks like your families are arriving," I said. "Since this is our last summer school class I want you to know how much I've enjoyed being your teacher. The three of you are exceptional students."

"We think you're an exceptional teacher," said Tommy.

"With a pretty exceptional horse," added Freedom, winking.

I swallowed hard, surprised by the swell of emotions I felt. "I hope you have a wonderful Fourth of July and I look forward to seeing you next school year."

"You better still be teaching, Mr. Revere," said Cam. "Or my mom will hunt Principal Sherman down and give him a piece of her mind." Again, we all laughed.

"Do you need a ride home?" Tommy asked Cam.

"Nah, my mom is coming to pick me up; thanks anyway," said Cam.

"By the way, did you find Little Liberty?" Tommy asked Liberty.

"He is safe back in Lexington," said Liberty, "munching on a big bag of grain."

"Awesome," replied Tommy. "See ya," he said as he raced off to his car.

Without saying anything, Freedom hugged Liberty around the neck. They stared at each other before Freedom hugged Liberty again. "Bye, Mr. Revere," said Freedom. "Life sure would be boring without American history."

"Amen," I said. "And keep painting. I want to see other moments in history through your eyes."

"I will, for sure," said Freedom as she waved a final time and dashed for her ride.

"I think life would be boring without Pop Rocks," said Liberty. "Seriously, have you tried those? Wow! When I ordered the lollipops online they threw in a small box of Pop Rocks. Those things are zippy!"

"Wait, you actually ordered something online?" Cam asked, surprised.

"Well, of course! I use voice control on Rush Revere's computer. I can't very well walk into a candy store and order from the counter."

"Good point," Cam said, nodding.

Cam and I received a text at the same time. I looked at my phone and saw it was from Danielle. It read:

> Cam & Mr. Revere. I lost track of time and now I'm late for an impt appt. I'll be back in an hour. Hoping Mr. Revere can take you home when you finish your class. Thanks. See you soon Cam. Can't wait for us to be a family tonight.

"Awesome!" Cam replied after reading his text.

"Have you tried Pop Rocks, too?" Liberty asked, clueless about the text message.

"No," said Cam. "I don't have to go home right away. We could go on another adventure."

"Are you thinking what I'm thinking?" I asked Cam, who was smiling.

"Are you thinking what I'm thinking?" Cam asked me. Of course, I was smiling as well.

"I want to be thinking what you guys are thinking but all I can think about is food," said Liberty.

I fed Liberty a couple of carrots and pulled myself onto Liberty's saddle. Cam jumped up behind me.

Liberty finished his carrots and said, "Well, I know what this means! I better get moving!"

"Right again!" I said.

John Adams was a statesman, diplomat, and a leading advocate
of American independence from Great Britain. He was also
the second president of the United States of America.

Liberty starting moving forward at a good pace and said, *"Rush, rush, rushing to history."* The time portal opened, and with my feet firmly in the stirrups, I yelled, "July 4th, 1776, the Pennsylvania State House, Philadelphia." We galloped toward the time portal and jumped into the past.

Liberty landed under the shadow of a large oak tree and alongside a small brick building. It appeared our arrival had gone unnoticed. As we moved around the small building I immediately recognized the large statehouse, now known as Independence Hall. It was a majestic looking building constructed from red bricks. Along the front and sides were many large windows trimmed in white. However, the most impressive part was the large bell tower and white steeple that reached up into the deep blue sky.

"Welcome to Independence Hall," I said.

"Awesome," replied Cam. "Should we go inside now?"

"Liberty, you realize you'll need to . . ." I said.

Liberty harrumphed. "I know, I know. I can't go inside. I'll wait out here and warn you if anyone tries to storm the castle!" he said sarcastically.

Soon Cam and I approached Independence Hall. We paused at the side of a cobblestone road to let a horse and carriage pass by. As we reached the front of the building, I opened the heavy wooden door and we entered into the large hallway. We walked along the smooth hardwood floors as we followed the many voices that led us to the distinguished gathering of our Founding Fathers.

We quietly slipped into a hidden corner at the back of the room. The room was filled with more than fifty men, most sitting on velvet-covered wooden chairs. There were five men standing in the middle of the room around a large desk.

Cam whispered, "Hey, that looks like Mr. Hancock, sitting behind that desk."

Sure enough, Cam was right! The last time we saw the Patriot leader was when we went to the Hancock-Clarke House with Paul Revere to warn Hancock and Samuel Adams that the British were coming to capture them! So much had happened since the Battle of Lexington.

I felt my heart pounding in my chest—I couldn't believe that this was the actual Congress and we were here!

"Why is Mr. Hancock sitting behind that desk?" asked Cam.

I spoke as softly as possible. "John Hancock is the representative from the colony of Massachusetts. He was elected as the president of the Continental Congress," I replied. "If you look at the Declaration of Independence document, you will see that John Hancock's name is the largest signature at the bottom."

"Who are those other men and why are they standing up?" Cam asked.

"Oh, they are all on the five-man committee that was assigned to draft the Declaration of Independence. They all gave their opinion on what should be kept in the document and what should be left out. Those brave men are the very same Patriots who wrote the lines that Liberty recited by the flagpole," I replied.

I was so excited and thrilled to be sharing this moment with Cam. This was a history teacher's dream come true. I was like a child at Disneyland.

"Can you guess which one is Thomas Jefferson?"

This is John Hancock, looking relaxed.
He signed his name in large print on the Declaration of Independence.

Cam looked thoughtful. "Um, is he the tall man with the reddish hair holding the document?"

"Yes, that's him!" I blurted out in a louder voice than I intended. "Oh my! That must be the actual Declaration of Independence in his hand. This is absolutely incredible!"

Cam looked at me sideways, probably thinking his teacher was a little bit nuts.

"Do you recognize the older man with the longer white hair beside him?" I asked after composing myself a bit.

"It looks like Benjamin Franklin, right?" Cam whispered. "I never got a chance to meet him but I remember how funny it was when Tommy told me that Liberty brought him back to Manchester Middle by mistake!" Cam laughed, holding his hand up to cover his mouth.

I whispered back, "I'm still trying to forget that ever happened." I refocused on the five men and asked, "How about the shorter man there on the front right, standing in front of John Hancock's chair?"

"Hmm, I'm not sure about him," Cam said, lifting up on his tiptoes to see better. "I know it's not Patrick Henry. I'd recognize him, anywhere."

"I'll give you a hint, his last name is Adams."

"Samuel Adams? The guy that was with John Hancock in Lexington?" Cam guessed.

"Good guess but no," I answered. "That is the future second President of the United States, John Adams—Samuel Adams's cousin. We met him when we visited the First Continental Congress awhile back. John Adams worked closely with Benjamin Franklin to edit Thomas Jefferson's writing of the Declaration of Independence."

Thomas Jefferson was an American Founding Father, the main author of the
Declaration of Independence, and the third president of the United States.

The Second Continental Congress meets to debate the
Declaration of Independence in 1776. The five men selected

to draft the document were John Adams, Benjamin Franklin,
Thomas Jefferson, Robert Livingston, and Roger Sherman.

I explained to Cam that it was really amazing to have representatives from different colonies all in the same room. In those days it took a long time to get from one place to another; there were no airplanes to make it a quick commute. Jefferson was from Virginia, Adams was from Massachusetts, and Franklin was from Pennsylvania. The other men standing were Robert Livingston of New York and Roger Sherman of Connecticut.

"So, they all wrote it?" Cam asked.

"Yes, they all contributed, but Thomas Jefferson is known as the main writer. Congress wanted to make sure that all colonies were represented," I said.

I thought at some point Cam might get bored but he remained intently focused. Just then a loud debate began. One member of Congress stood and began to speak in favor of the declaration; another then stood and spoke against it. The debate started to become heated.

"What are they arguing about? Aren't they all on the same side?" Cam asked with a confused look on his face.

"Yes, they are, but they have different views about what is best for their own colony and the thirteen colonies together. When war first broke out most Americans did not want to fight Great Britain. The battles at Lexington and Concord along with Thomas Paine's *Common Sense* changed that thinking. A month ago Congressman Richard Henry Lee introduced a motion calling for independence. This sparked a massive debate!"

"And they're still arguing after a month? That's crazy!" Cam said.

One congressman looked like he would come to blows with another, but John Hancock demanded that they both sit down.

"Yes, it was a very serious thing to declare independence. It

Do you know what this important document is? Along with the Bill of Rights and the U.S. Constitution, the Declaration of Independence is one of the most important American documents. It was written by Thomas Jefferson with the help of John Adams and Benjamin Franklin.

meant if America lost the war, these men, the signers of the Declaration of Independence, would likely all be put to death!"

"Wow, that's serious," said Cam.

I nodded and said, "The Declaration was the first of its kind.
Never before in the history of the world have a country's people
written a document declaring their right to choose their own
government."

John Hancock reached over and gently took the Declaration
of Independence from Thomas Jefferson. John Adams placed his
hand on his hip and leaned in while Benjamin Franklin crossed
his arms on his chest. Hancock scratched onto the document,
raising and lowering his hand. He put down the quill pen and
blew on the wet ink.

"This is an incredibly important moment in our history. The
Declaration of Independence became one of the three most
famous and important official documents of the United States,
along with the Constitution and Bill of Rights," I said. "Remember, America did not become truly independent until years later,
in 1783. There were many more battles to come until the Americans finally won the war."

Cam kept staring at what was happening in the middle of the
room. Then he sneakily pulled his phone from his pocket and
used me as a shield as he cautiously snapped a picture of this
life-changing, historical event.

"The Declaration of Independence is really America's promise
of a government of the people, where everyone is equal and free.
You know, Cam, one of the reasons that this moment is so special is that the men and women in our armed forces and in our
government today are still fighting and sacrificing for the very
same rights that these men are arguing about right here."

Suddenly Cam turned to me and energetically said, "Mr. Revere, it all makes sense now. We have to go back to modern day right away!" he said.

What was it that finally made sense to him? Whatever it was, it seemed very important. Cam was pulling me by my coat sleeve back into the hallway. As we exited the room he was nearly running to the door. I had a hard time keeping up. As he reached the door, I noticed something was wrong. Cam's eyebrows were scrunched and he seemed to be lost in his own thoughts. "Is everything all right?" I asked, wondering what I had said that made him want to bolt to the door. "Are you feeling sick?"

We slipped out of Independence Hall and raced back to where we left Liberty. Oddly enough, he was at the base of the large tree with a bird balancing on his nose.

"What are you doing?" I asked. "We need to time-jump back to the future right now."

"Okay, okay," said Liberty. "Excuse me for saving a young bird that fell out of its nest." Liberty reached his nose to one of the lower branches. Sure enough, there was a bird's nest that rested at the intersection of two limbs. Liberty gently placed the bird back in the nest. It chirped and flapped its wings.

"I wish I had something to feed it," said Liberty.

"I don't think it's hungry," I said. "I think it's ready to leave the nest."

"And I really need to leave 1776," said Cam.

"Okay, I'm ready," Liberty said as I hoisted myself onto his saddle. "But for the record, I think you should start carrying fresh worms in your pockets. I think that bird was hungry. Now I'm starting to get hungry. But not for worms. Blech. One time I found a worm while eating an apple. Double-blech! Do you know what's worse than finding a worm in your apple?" Liberty asked.

I could only imagine. "No, what?"

"Finding half a worm in your apple!" Liberty said with a big laugh.

I ignored him and asked Cam, "Do you want to try to meet up with your mom?"

"That would be great," said Cam. "But she didn't tell me where she was going. Her text didn't say, either. Only that it was important. Hey, maybe Liberty can track her down with his special radar ability."

"That only works with historical figures. I mean I've never tried tracking someone in modern day," said Liberty. "But I'll try." He closed his eyes and furrowed his brow. After a few seconds, he said. "Sorry, I'm not getting anything. Hmm, wait, I know. Maybe with Freedom's help, we could do it together. Her connection in modern day might do the trick. Stand by." Again, Liberty concentrated. Almost a full minute passed before Liberty said, "Bingo! We found her."

"Well, where is she?" I asked.

"She's at the airport," said Liberty.

"That's strange," Cam said.

"Liberty, are you sure Cam's mom is at the airport?"

"Positivo," Liberty confirmed.

"Can you take us there?" asked Cam.

"Did Henry Knox bring fifty-nine guns and cannons from Fort Ticonderoga?"

"What are we waiting for?" Cam said.

We jumped on the back of Liberty, who said, "*Rush, rush, rushing from history*."

* * *

Within seconds we were through the time portal and landed in the airport terminal parking lot. We dismounted from Liberty and quickly made plans to meet up at the same place later. Cam and I shuffled our way in between cars, through the sliding glass doors, and across the airport lobby to where dozens of people were waiting near the escalator. Many were holding "Welcome Home" signs and several were holding American flags of all sizes.

"Hey, there's my mom," Cam said. Sure enough, Danielle was standing with a couple of other families. She wore a patriotic-looking dress and was holding a small American flag. When Cam was a few feet away he yelled, "Mom!"

I stood back and watched what was about to unfold.

Danielle turned around and when she saw her son she looked utterly shocked. "What are you doing here?" she exclaimed.

"I was going to ask you the same thing, but I think I know. Is Dad coming home?"

Danielle smiled and for a second I thought she was going to cry. She said, "He is. I was going to surprise you but it looks like you—"

Before she could finish, Cam wrapped his arms around his mother and said, "I'm so sorry, Mom. I was such a jerk. I've learned a lot with Mr. Revere. He brought me to the airport. . . . Anyway, I understand now."

Just then the crowd started clapping and cheering for the first passengers descending on the escalator. Men and women in military uniforms and carrying heavy backpacks descended in single file. As they stepped off the escalator and into the arms of their loved ones I couldn't help but get emotional. I could feel some tears building in my eyes.

I had never seen Cam's dad but it was easy to pick him out. Same brown eyes, same strong chin, same wide smile that lit up the lobby. When his father was only halfway down the escalator, Cam hurried to wait at the bottom. He stared up at his father and saluted. I could tell the sight of his son brought a wave of emotions. He stepped off the escalator and wrapped Cam in his arms, lifting him off his feet.

I stood behind a nearby pillar and watched the happy reunion. Cam's mom joined in and hugged her husband tight.

"Hey, bud, wow, you've grown. What have you been eating?"

"Just Mom's awesome cooking," said Cam. "I bet you can't wait for some of your favorite lasagna." Cam's father looked lovingly at Danielle.

His dad tossed his backpack to the floor and put both hands on his son's shoulders. He looked into his eyes and said, "I really missed you. I know it's been hard on you this last year. I'm sorry I had to go."

"It's okay, Dad, I understand," Cam said.

"Most of the time I was in Afghanistan I was working, but when I sat down at night I thought of you and what you were up to back home."

"Really, I know, Dad, I understand everything," Cam said.

"I know I don't say this enough but I'm proud of you and love you very much, Cam. Are you still mad at me?"

Cam replied, "No, really, I'm not. I was just so sad and confused when you left, it made me angry. I had no idea what made you leave us. Why you had to go so far away and miss all my games and stuff. But I understand now." Cam smiled.

"You keep saying you understand. What do you mean?" Cam's dad smiled at Danielle and hugged her again.

Cam said, "I understand why you left us. You went to fight for our country so we could be safe at home. You went away to protect us like the first American soldiers did. You went to defend our freedoms written in the Declaration of Independence."

"Wow, that's right, son. I'm impressed. Not only are you bigger, but you're a lot more mature."

"I went to visit the Battle of Lexington, and I met George Washington, and I had to dodge bullets and cannonballs and fight the Redcoats! I talked to a soldier in the first American army. He told me all about how he had to leave his family to fight the British so that we could have a free country."

Cam's father looked thoroughly amused and glanced at his wife. She smiled serenely and Cam's father laughed loudly. "Ha! That is so cool," he said. "I am so glad you've discovered American history and like it so much. I'd love to meet George Washington. He was an incredible leader back in his day."

Cam laughed, "Yeah, American history is awesome. I've learned a lot from it. Mom probably told you I got in a fight with this big kid named Billy. He's always bugging me. But guess what, Dad? After the Battle of Lexington and the Battle of Concord and visiting with Paul Revere and George Washington I got some ideas on how to be smarter even though Billy had my team really outnumbered."

"You visited with Paul Revere and George Washington?" asked Cam's dad, who smiled and glanced at Cam's mom again.

"Yeah," said Cam, "and Dr. Joseph Warren at Bunker Hill. He almost inoculated me for smallpox. But that's another story. And John Hancock and Samuel Adams, and his cousin John Adams and, of course, Benjamin Franklin. Seriously, though, they were all Patriots and heroes just like you! They did everything they could to keep the dream of the Pilgrims alive. Without heroes like them I doubt we could've ever separated from Great Britain so we could be our own country. All the signers of the Declaration of Independence were really brave. They knew they were putting themselves in danger by signing their autographs. All these men knew they might be leaving their family forever, but they did it anyway. They were amazing! Our history is amazing!"

"Son, *you* are amazing! Your enthusiasm and passion is what makes America great. Never forget that," he said as he playfully messed up Cam's hair.

"I never will, Dad. I promise."

"I love you, son." Cam's father lifted his bag and slung it over his shoulder. He grabbed Cam around the shoulder with one hand and with the other he pulled his wife close to him. Together, father, mother, and son walked toward the airport doors, heading home.

Cam's mom looked back as if hoping to catch a familiar face. When she saw me she waved over her shoulder and smiled brightly.

My heart swelled as I, too, walked outside and saw Cam's family stroll into the morning sun, underneath a large American flag, billowing in the wind.

"Psst! Over here!" said Liberty from behind a nearby tree.

"I knew you were around here somewhere," I said. "Did you stay out of trouble?"

"Well, of course. I'm always extra good on July Fourth," said Liberty, smiling.

"So, what do you want to do for the rest of the day?" I asked, thinking I already knew the answer.

"You mean besides eating at an all-you-can-eat vegetable buffet?"

"Yes, I mean after that."

"How about a nice long nap and then we can stay up for the fireworks show! Maybe plan our next adventure?"

I smiled and nodded. "Sounds perfect."

And it was.

Cameron represents the thousands of children nationwide
with family members serving our country. We know it is not easy at
times, but we are so proud of you! This young man is named Shaun,
sent in by his mother, Leanne B., to www.RushRevere.com.

Acknowledgments

Thank you first and foremost to all the selfless men and women of our armed forces. You and your families truly sacrifice every single day and we are eternally grateful.

This Adventure Series is a labor of love with a mission to share the incredible stories of our founding in a unique and creative way. I want every child in the United States and around the world to learn what it means to be an American and what American Exceptionalism is really all about. Thank you for embracing this series and honoring us with your fan emails, letters, and photos.

I could not do this alone and thank the extraordinary team assembled around me. My wife, Kathryn, is the unwavering and passionate mastermind behind this entire project. She dedicated countless hours to making sure this is not just a book, but also a heartfelt experience for all. She is exceptionally bright, talented, detailed, and immensely caring, which shows in everything she does.

Jonathan Adams Rogers is our right hand on this entire project and it simply would not be what it is without him. He is devoted to excellence and goes the extra mile and does every-thing that is needed to ensure that goal is reached. He does all that he can. And then a little more.

Thank you to Penelope Adams Rogers for your inspiring cre-ativity and for your sharp attention to detail.

A big thank-you also goes out to Chris Schoebinger and Christopher Hiers for making sure the vision comes to life in a way that children can appreciate. Your talent and illustrations are tremendous!

David Limbaugh, Louise Burke, and Mitchell Ivers, and every-one at Simon & Schuster, thank you from the bottom of our hearts for your support and efforts to make this series a success.

A wonderful view of America with young patriots Todd and Mallie.

Photo Credits

116	Christopher Hiers
130	Christopher Hiers
132	Jonathan Adams Rogers
136	Christopher Hiers
145	Christopher Hiers
154	Wikimedia Commons
156	Wikimedia Commons
162	Christopher Hiers
165	Christopher Hiers
174–75	Wikimedia Commons
182	Christopher Hiers
188	Christopher Hiers
194	Wikimedia Commons
197	© Lee Snider/Photo Images/Corbis
201	Wikimedia Commons
202	National Portrait Gallery, gift of Henry Willett, 1892 via Wikimedia Commons
208	Christopher Hiers
214	Christopher Hiers
222	Wikimedia Commons
225	Museum of Fine Arts, Boston, Wikimedia Commons
227	Wikimedia Commons
228–29	Wikimedia Commons
231	Wikimedia Commons
240	Leanne B.
242	Sara Y.